# WRATH

## A DEADLY SINS MC NOVELLA

### KAY MAREE

Contents

WRATH

A DEADLY SINS MC NOVELLA

**First edition. October, 2018.**

Copyright © 2018 KAY MAREE.



Written by Kay Maree

Disclaimer

This story is a figment of the author's imagination.

All characters are fictional and are not intended to represent anyone living or dead.

# Prologue

***Two Months Earlier...***

"What ya doing girl?" Ava asks into my ear as I park my car in front of my sister, Julie's place. Turning the car off, I prepare myself to battle the rain coming down. Jumping out, I shut the door with my hip and ducking my head at the same time as the rain splashes onto my face, I race to the awning above the entrance door to her building.

"Just stopped at Julie's," I breathlessly answer while pushing the glass door open.

"Do you mind asking her what the title of that book was, please?"

I roll my eyes at her pleading voice. "Okay, why didn't you ask her last week?"

"I did. She told me but I forgot."

Her reply makes me laugh.

"You're bloody hopeless." I push my drenched hair out of my face.

"Shut up, you," she hisses playfully, making me laugh again as I trudge up the chilly stairwell towards Julie's apartment.

"Okay, I'll ask," I reassure her before hanging up and pocketing my phone.

Pulling my key out, I unlock the door and step inside.

"Honey, I'm home!" I call out to Julie, but she doesn't reply.

Normally, she'll call back, reminding me this isn't my place. But, it's dead silent. Her car was in her usual park so she should be here. Scrunching my eyebrows up in confusion, I make my way towards her room, thinking she may be in the shower. Pushing her door open, I freeze and feel the blood pumping through my veins turn ice cold.

"Julie!" I scream, finally finding my voice.

I dash to her side, fall to my knees and gather her limp body in my arms.

"Julie, come on sis, wake up!" I shake in fear and tears pour from my eyes, making everything blurry. Reaching into my pocket for the phone, I pull it out and punch in ooo. I rest it between my shoulder and chin waiting for it to connect, all the while begging her to wake up.

I glance around the room and I notice what looks like a syringe lying on the floor at the same moment someone on the other end of the phone speaks to me. Turning back to check Julie, I notice her arm and the piece of rubber tied tightly around it.

"No, no, no, no, this can't be happening."

The woman on the phone shouts to get my attention. Through wrenching sobs, I try to explain what is going on.

***

As I watch my sister being lifted onto the gurney by the paramedics, I reach for her hand and feel how cold to the touch she is.

"Ma'am we need to move her, now." The soft voice penetrates my head and all I can do is nod before following them out. When we step onto the street, I reach into my pocket, pull out my phone and press call on the first number that comes up on my screen. I'm not even sure who I'm actually calling as I climb into the back of the ambulance. Hearing a soft voice answer my call, I simply answer, "Julie."

"What's wrong?" Alexis' voice clears my mind and through my sobs I manage to tell her what's happening.

A numbing feeling settles deep in my bones and before she can reply, I end the call. To be honest, I'm not sure if she understood a word I just said. Everything seems so methodical, like I'm on autopilot.

The ambulance pulls to a sharp stop, I register the doors being pulled open and then Julie is raced into the ED. Someone is talking to me, leading me into a building. I think it's a nurse but my brain has seemed to shut off. I feel like I'm in a tunnel, voices echo around me and they could be speaking English or gibberish for all I know. Everything around me seems to be unraveling. The pieces and threads of every happy memory we've ever shared together, shatters around me in disarray. It could be moments or, even hours later, that I'm ushered into a small room. I take nothing in as the beating of my heart echoes around me.

A middle-aged man in a white coat enters the room. "Harlow Rodgers?"

He's holding a clipboard and has a grave look on his face. Even before he speaks, I know what he is about to say.

"I'm sorry."

It's all he gets out before a raw, agonized cry tears from my throat. Tears fall thick and fast down my cheeks. Wrapping my arms around my waist, I try to ward off the chill which has blanketed me. My heart feels like it's being shredded into tiny pieces. I watch as his mouth moves, but I've lost the ability to hear or even speak. My mouth is dry, my breaths are coming in pants, numbness overtakes every one of my senses.

*This can't be happening,* I repeat over and over again, as if my words alone could be strong enough for the news to be undone. Feeling like the walls are closing in on me, I move past the doctor without a word. His voice sounds far away as he calls out to me, but I don't stop. I keep walking until I reach the sliding glass doors which lead outside.

Stepping outside, I breathe in the fresh clean scent as rain pours down around me. My body is gripped by despair so strong it's hard to breathe. I feel like I've become a prisoner in my own body and no matter what I do, I'll never escape it. I'll never be free again. Giving in, I fall to my knees onto the rain-kissed footpath and let it consume me.

"Harlow, we have you," someone calls out.

Arms wrap around me; multiple voices cocoon me. In the deep recesses of my mind, I allow their warmth and soft words to soothe me even if it's only for a short while.

# Chapter One

**Harlow**

Tapping my long, red tipped nails on the wooden table in front of me, I stare at the invite card. Picking it up, I flip it over and over in one hand while I hold the phone with the other. I read the print over again, making sure I have the details correct. Working at the Ivy club for the past month waiting for this event to happen has finally paid off. I read the card yet again..........

**Be Seduced...**

**7 Deadly Sins**

**1 Tempting Affair**

**May 6th 2018, 9pm**

**Hosted by Deadly Sins MC & Club Ivy Newcastle**

**All proceeds go to The Cancer foundation**

**Be Bad, Be Good**

**Pick your flavour...**

"Harlow, are you listening to me?" My best friend, Tilly shouts into my ear.

I drop the card to the table in front of me so I can concentrate on the phone conversation.

"Yep, I'm here."

I hear her blow out a frustrated breath, she knows full well I didn't hear a word she just said. "Listen I love ya like my own sister, but you can't just rock up to this party by yourself. For fuck sake, it's run by biker's and not just any biker's, but fucking 1%er's"

"Tilly, I need to go. I need answers and you know me better than anyone. I can't just sit on my fucking hands and do nothing"

"Shit! Shit! Shit! That's the problem, I *do* know you. You're too bloody stubborn for your own good. It doesn't matter what me and the girl's say, you're going to do what you want and that scares the shit out of me."

I get that she's worried but this is something I need to do. "What if it was your sister?" I know full well, she wouldn't sit idly by.

"Fine," she huffs after a moment of silence. "But me and the girls are coming with you."

"Um, no..." That's all I manage before she cuts me off.

"So..." I can picture her hands on her hips like they usually are when she uses that tone of voice and try not to giggle. "You're telling me, if I was in your shoes, you wouldn't demand to come with me?"

Yeah, she's got me. I wouldn't even have to think about it. There's no way I'd allow her to go alone. "Fine. You win but don't drag the girls into this."

"Too late. If you hadn't been ignoring our group chat for the past day or so you would have seen our messages about which sinful outfit we're each wearing."

"What do you mean?" I sound confused because I am.

"The party's theme is 7 Deadly Sins, right? So, as there are seven of us, we've decided each of us will dress as a different sin."

"Of course, you have." I'm not sure how I feel about this.

"Don't get all fucking grumpy about it, we have this shit sorted. Deal with it."

"What's my sin?" I change the subject, knowing she's getting pissed with me.

"What else – Wrath." She giggles.

I must admit, it sounds perfect right at this moment. I feel the anger about what happened to my sister slice through me like a hot knife.

"We'll meet at your place tomorrow arvo around three and don't stress about your outfit, Peyton and I are going to pick them all up today."

"I don't know about this," I mumble before rubbing my forehead with my free hand. I feel a headache coming on. I'm worried about dragging my friends into something which could get them hurt.

"Julie was like our sister too, Harlow. We agreed to always be there for each other so, shut up and let's get this shit done." Her voice starts out hard before becoming soft.

I can tell she's trying hard not to cry. Swallowing past the lump in my throat, I attempt to speak. "Okay," I concede.

"Love ya, girl."

"Love ya, too," I say before clicking 'end call.'

Dropping my phone to the table, I eye the invite again and shake off the emotions from the call. I push away from the table, head into the small kitchenette and grab a glass of water. I grab my phone again, pull up the group text and scroll through what the girls wrote last night.

Shaking my head at their stubbornness, I drop my phone back to the table and head upstairs to have a shower.

Turning the taps on, I strip out of my work clothes and jump under the hot spray. Lifting my face to the hot water, images of my sister replay over and over. Images from the night I called by her home to be confronted with her lifeless body, lying crumpled on the bedroom floor. From the day our parents died, I promised I would protect her. I failed her when she was alive and now the reality that her life has been taken away is like a slap in the face. I will not fail her again.

I feel tears well behind my closed lids and will them not to fall, it doesn't work. As the tears spill free down my cheeks, I don't do anything to stop them. This is the one time I will allow myself to feel this way. My heart feels like it's caged in a vice, squeezing it tighter and tighter with each exhale. Strong grief slams through me, holding my soul captive and I know this feeling will probably remain with me for the rest of my life.

I slam my hands against the tiles hard enough to send pain ricocheting up my arms. I allow the pain to ground me as my mind swirls with uncertainties as to why this happened to my sweet little sister. How the hell did she end up dead when she was the one who always did things right? I've always been the one to push the boundaries. We were like chalk and cheese.

Julie was the bookworm type and *I* was the party girl. This shit just isn't adding up in my head, but by this time tomorrow night, I *will* have the answers I need. I'll kill the person who took my sister away from me. I swear to all that is holy in this world – I will make them pay. For now, I'll let this gut wrenching grief rip me apart and consume me. Tomorrow, I'll pull my shit together and get the vengeance my sister deserves.

***

It's almost six in the evening and I have managed to center myself for what's to come. Stepping out of the shower, I wrap a towel around myself. Beads of water linger on my warm skin. I hurry to my bedside table, fighting off the chill in the air of my bedroom. Reaching down, I click the 'on' button on my iPod dock. After a moment of silence, Julie's playlist begins and I let *Like a Prayer* by *Madonna* soak through me. I head back into the small attached ensuite and rest my hands against the bathroom sink. Bowing my head, I suck in a few deep calming breaths and will all the strength I possess to push me through the hurt that's constantly squeezing the life out of me. Pushing the grief aside, I let the anger I've been bottling up for the past two months, simmer in my veins. Slowly lifting my face, I stare at my reflection in the mirror -

light brown hair with honey coloured streaks, dark brown eyes which follow a slender pierced nose to my tattoo covered chest. Above a set of wings is tattooed, 'true love.' The wings lead to the middle of my chest and a heart. There's a cross covered with vines and roses, 'forever' is written in the centre. Turning my right arm and holding it out, I take in the intricate detail of the gun and rose with vines traveling down to my hand. Returning my gaze to the mirror, I admire the two new doves on each side of my neck. In memory of Julie.

For most of my life, I've been considered different. Pushing back against society and what they deem appropriate but I've always been a happy-go-lucky girl. Sure, I was a bit on the wild side and filled with sass, but I have always been polite. Tonight, that changes. Polite goes out the fucking window. Tonight, I will be the baddest bitch anybody has ever encountered. I don't give a fuck what I have to do to get justice to my sister. Whoever did this is going to wish they'd never been born - in my eyes they're already fucking dead.

Nodding to my mirror image, I turn the tap on at the sink and splash cold water on my face. I reach blindly beside me for a hand-towel and grabbing it, I wipe the water from my face. I hear voices, it's my friends entering my apartment. I sigh and shake my head. Their loud as fuck voices carry over the music blaring in my room. After dropping the hand towel onto the sink, I adjust the fluffy bath towel around my chest. I hear footsteps on the stairs but they fade when the girls reach the carpeted hallway which leads to my room.

*The girls have arrived in force!* I smile to myself, secretly relieved and equal parts annoyed, that they're here. I didn't want to drag them into this shit, I was fearful they'd be hurt. I'm relieved I won't be alone though. The girls have my back.

"Yo, Chicka." Callie's voice sing songs over the music as she enters my room. "Are you ready for a sinful night?" She wiggles her eyebrows at me when I open the bathroom door with the towel wrapped around me.

I take in her black and white Playboy bodysuit with bunny ears and bowtie. It's complimented by black fishnet stockings and her favorite pair of black Maryjane spiked heels.

"Shit girl, let me guess. You're *Lust.*"

I laugh when she winks before giving me a little curtsey, turning around so I can see the bunny tail and giving her Jennifer Lopez ass a shake.

"Right you are baby-cakes. Now, throw on a robe and come check the other girls out downstairs. You need to grab your outfit for the night."

She thumbs over her shoulder and I hear the girls' laughter coming from the living room downstairs. There's the loud pop of what I assume is a wine bottle being opened.

"Hurry your ass up, I think the girls are starting without us." The words are thrown over her shoulder as she makes her way from my room. I hurriedly drop my towel and throw on the robe which was lying on the foot of my bed. I follow her down the hallway, her long black hair swings from side to side as she hurries downstairs

I need to talk to the girls again, to make sure they are serious about tonight and remind them of the risks involved. Making my way to the living room, I can't hide the smile which graces my lips at the sight of my friends all dressed up. Ava hands me a freshly poured glass of white wine. I don't usually like wine but I'll have a glass every now and then with the girls.

"Thanks."

Tilly draws my attention. "Can you guess each of our sins?"

Taking a mouthful of wine, I try not to scrunch up my face at the horrid taste before looking at each of the girls.

"These aren't costumes," I laugh. "They're more like glorified underwear," I say in mock horror, making them all laugh.

"Okay. I already guessed that Callie is *Lust*."

Callie shakes her hips again and we giggle.

"Tilly, you resemble Poison Ivy. You must be *Envy*. Peyton you look like a sexy poker player so, you must be *Greed*." I glance at Ava and note the cute little apron. "Ava," I laugh. "You look like a slutty chef, you're *Gluttony*. Alexis, since you're the queen of living in your pajamas it doesn't surprise me that you're *Sloth* in your cute little blue nightie." I wink at her. "That leaves us with *Pride* for Holly."

"Smartass, go and get your outfit on." Holly hands me a white bag with *Sinful Nights* stamped across the front.

"Really?" I eye the bag in her hands. "You went to the sex shop to get our outfits?" I bite back a laugh.

"I thought it suited the theme of the night." Payton shrugs with a mischievous smirk.

"I bet," I muse. "We're going to look like fucking strippers." I groan, really worrying about their thought process.

"Yeah, but at least we'll look like high priced strippers." Tilly traps her bottom lip between her teeth, trying not to laugh.

"Come on, go and get ready. I bet you'll love what we got for you." Payton nudges me with her shoulder. Taking the bag, I pause for a moment. I need to make sure they know what they're getting themselves into. As much as it's all fun and games, getting dressed up and partying, this isn't just another party to me. This is serious business.

"As much as I appreciate each of you girls wanting to come tonight, I want you to really think about this first. It isn't just some regular party we're going to tonight, this is where I find the justice Julie deserves" I breathe out a hard breath, needing them to understand how serious I am. "I don't think I could live with myself if one of you girls got hurt." I look each of them in the eye.

"Nothing will stop us going tonight," Alexis says adamantly.

"We've had each other's backs since the day we met in primary school, this doesn't change anything," Ava answers.

Nodding, I understand what they are saying but, need them to understand how serious this is. "When I walk in there tonight, I may not come back out."

A sudden tension settles over the room as the girls think about what I have just said. After a few moments Tilly breaks the silence.

"Would you walk in there with one of us, even knowing the risks?" Tilly slams her hands on her hips. After all these years of knowing each other, I can't lie to them. I want to, but before I can say a word, Holly speaks.

"Have the police been in contact, have they found anything new?" Holly murmurs.

I shake my head. "They're not telling me anything new. Same shit, different day." My voice takes on a hard edge. I don't mean to sound pissy. I know the police have done everything in their power. They can only go on the evidence they have and it's not a lot. As it stands at the moment, it looks like she was given a hotshot. There was no proof anybody else was with her, but I know my sister – she had a hatred for drugs, she would never put that shit in her body.

"So, I ask again. Would you walk in there with one of us even when you know the risks?" Tilly asks softer this time, pulling me from my thoughts.

"Yes."

"Then there's nothing else to discuss." Callie places her hands on my shoulders and turns me towards the stairs. "Go and get your ass ready while I grab you a beer out of the fridge, don't think I didn't see you scrunch up your nose at the taste of the wine."

"Damn, I thought I did really good covering it up."

Laughing at my retreating back, she calls out, "Nope."

Shaking my head, I gnaw on my bottom lip, knowing there is no way to convince them not to come with me. Maybe we can hang out for a few hours then, I'll make my break and try to find out as much information as I can without getting them involved.

Closing my bedroom door, I lean my back against the cool wood of the door and try to steady myself. I'm worried as hell about what might happen to my friends tonight, but no matter what I say to them, I know they're as hard headed as me. It won't matter what I say, they won't listen.

Pushing off the door, I cross to the volume control on the dock and turn it up. *Meant to Be* by *Bebe Rexha (feat. Florida. Georgia Line)* starts to play. I get lost in the lyrics as I remove the robe start to get ready. The outfit is literally lingerie. *Damn these girls, this is the last bloody time I let them organise the costumes.*

Staring at myself in the full-length mirror, I take in the strapless latex dress with a sweetheart neckline. It flares out at the hips, hitting mid-thigh. The hemline is cut to look like flames are flowing down my thighs. Red strips of silk are sewn underneath so it hangs about an inch longer than the black latex, it's off center a little so you can see the silk. It's actually quite sexy. I slip on black seamless knickers and fishnet stockings. I release my hair from a butterfly clip and let it cascade down my back naturally, giving it a bed-hair look. Heading into the bathroom, I grab my eyeliner from the top drawer of my vanity along with mascara, black eyeshadow and my red lipstick. Applying the eyeliner, mascara and eyeshadow, I make sure I get a smoky-eye look. Running the tip of my nail under the liquid eyeliner on my top lid, I make sure the lines flick out equally on each side. Grabbing the cherry red lipstick, I apply a decent amount and smack my lips together. I'm satisfied I have the look I was going for. Sexy, but a girl not to be messed with. Heading back to the bedroom,

I grab my black Doc boots and sit on the edge of my bed to pull them on and lace them up. I throw one last look at myself in the mirror and hum, satisfied I'm ready to go.

# Chapter Two

**Drake**

Rolling the glass tumbler of scotch around with the tips of my fingers, I study the man who is basically shitting his pants in front of me. He's flanked by Pyro and Razor so, I totally understand how he feels. Pyro is built like a brick fucking shithouse and Razor is just as big. I toss back the last mouthful of scotch and feel the familiar burn as it slices down my throat. Lifting the heavy file in front of me, I kick my heavy boots up onto the edge of the old desk with a thud. Leaning back in the wooden chair so it balances on two legs; I flip the file open, light up a smoke and suck in a deep inhale.

"Trevor, I didn't think even you would be this fucking stupid." I eye the weasel of a man who thought he could fucking steal from us. His face is as white as the paper in front of me. I bite back a chuckle when his throat bobs up and down on a deep swallow.

"Mercy, it's not what you think." His voice cracks as he pleads.

I hold up my hand, I'm really getting fucked off now at this piece of shit. I open my mouth to say something but my phone cuts in.

"Get this piece of shit out of my face," I grunt to my man as I reach for the phone.

"Trevor, don't go too far, we haven't finished yet." I growl between clenched teeth, not bothering to meet his eyes before I look at the screen. Prez's name flashes up.

"Prez?"

"Drake did you sort the shit out?" That's Prez for ya, straight to the fucking point. No beating around the fucking bush.

"Pyro is keeping him close while I sort through the files." I breath out deeply, blowing smoke out when I do.

"Where the fuck are Shadow and Crank? They're the fucking secretary and treasurer, they should be doing this shit."

"They should be there any minute."

"Good."

"We need this shit sorted and fast, Drake. So, no fucking around, just get it done."

The entire fucking statement doesn't even deserve a fucking answer so, I suck down the anger swelling inside me before I speak again. "Are you swinging by tonight?"

"Nah brother, I still have my cousins kid here."

"Got it."

"Now, get this shit sorted, we have other things coming up that need our attention."

He doesn't even wait for a reply before hanging up. Taking another drag of my smoke, I flip the phone around in my hand before quickly tapping out a text to Razor – telling him to send Shadow and Crank up here as soon as they arrive.

Looking towards the numerous monitors lining the opposite wall, I watch as the *Club Ivy* staff start setting up for tonight's party. Every year the club picks a charity to donate money to and we host a party to collect as much as possible for them. As it stands, *Club Ivy* is one of only two places we own which is legitimate and we like to keep it that way. Fuckbag, Trevor, thought it fucking wise to not just steal from the club, but to also dip his greasy fucking hands into the money which has already been collected for the charity. He was brought in to run things for us, but after tonight he won't even have hands to wipe his own ass. And, that's just for starters. If everything goes to plan, by tomorrow morning he'll be pushing up fucking daisy's.

"VP!" Pyro barks out in an attempt to get my attention.

I snap my eyes to his, he fills the whole fucking doorway.

"What?" I grunt before returning my eyes back to the file in my lap.

"Razor is with Trevor, they're sorting shit out with the bar staff."

"Good, I want eyes on him all night. Shit is too fucking chaotic right now and I need either Crank or Shadow here to go through the numbers. We need to work out what else this fucker has taken."

I let my boots hit the floor with a thud and run a frustrated hand through my hair before reaching for the bottle of cheap fucking scotch and topping up my glass.

"I don't trust that piece of shit, brother," Pyro spits out. He flicks a *Zippo* lighter open and closed with his fingers.

"Same, so make sure he doesn't skip out on us." I take another mouthful of scotch and relish the burn as it works its way down my throat. I want nothing more than to break this bottle over that piece of shit's head.

***

I'm not sure how many fucking hours me and the boys have been at this shit, but I need a fucking break before my head explodes. Looking over to the monitors again, I note the party is in full swing. I scan from monitor to monitor, there's a camera placed in each of the seven rooms which have been set up for a different sin.

"I'm going to go check everything is good downstairs and make sure our little friend isn't giving Pyro the shits," I mutter to Shadow.

Crank lets out a low chuckle while still studying the file laying in front of him.

"You'll be lucky if he isn't dead already." Shadow glances up from the file in his hands. He's frowning, which is nothing new.

I swear, in all the time I've known the man, I've never seen him smile. Crank is the fucking complete opposite. Pushing to my feet, I stretch my back and cross towards the door.

"Pyro knows the score," I throw over my shoulder.

"You wanna hope your right, VP," Shadow mumbles just before I slam the door shut behind me.

I take the polished wooden stairs down to the lower level and nod to Dice who's standing at the bottom, making sure no one comes upstairs. He rolls a pair of dice in his hand, hence how he got the nickname -Dice.

Looking around, I take it all in. True to the name of the club, there are ivy vines chasing down every exposed brick wall with huge globe lights hanging from the massive ceiling. Glancing over towards the bar, I note the Club Ivy sign in bright neon green lights. It's in the middle of glass shelving which displays the best liquor available. There's also a stunning waterfall behind the glass wall of the display.

"Everything good, brother?" I ask Dice when I step up beside him. I notice his long black hair is tied back in a low ponytail.

"It's about as good as it can get." He chuckles and I watch as his eyes travel down a pair of tanned legs.

"Head in the fucking game tonight, Dice, we have shit to handle. Stay the fuck away from the Greed room."

"Don't worry, VP, my shit is in the game.". He has a knowing smirk on his face.

"Fuck," I mutter as I head to the bar. "Scotch straight up," I tell the guy behind the bar, but he's not listening. He's too fucking busy with his eyes glued to a pair of fake tits.

Slamming my hand down hard on the wooden bar, he finally snaps his eyes to me. He looks pissed at the fact I've interrupted him but the look quickly vanishes when he notices my cut.

"Coming straight up," he stammers out while grabbing the bottle of scotch.

"Fucking pussy," I mutter as he slides the glass over to me.

"Hey handsome." A woman's voice slurs next to me.

*Seriously? You're gonna fuck me with this shit tonight?* I blow out a rough breath.

"Not interested," I mutter before slamming back the drink.

"How about I suck you off, it might calm your ass down?" The chick sidles up closer to me. Her too strong perfume wafts up my nose, making my head spin. From the corner of my eye, I see her reach out to touch my arm but I grab it before she can make contact.

"How about you go find somebody else for the night?" I grit out.

I'm looking at her now and notice, not only are her eyes bloodshot, but her pupils are blown. I drag my gaze over her a bit closer – her too tight clothes are stretched across her fake tanned ass and I shake my head with disgust. Looking back to her blown eyes, I turn her arm over and take in the track marks. I drop her arm back to her side.

"Don't be like that, I'll make it real good for you."

I can't believe she's trying again. Is this bitch for real?

"How about you fuck off?"

I don't give her a chance to try again. Turning, I head for the front doors. I need a smoke and some fresh fucking air.

I'm thirty fucking years old and I don't do the club shit anymore. I don't mind sitting around the clubhouse and shooting the shit before taking one of the sweetbutts to bed though. It's just the way I like it - no attachments or commitments, except to my brothers. It's just less fucking complicated that way and I sure as hell don't dip my dick into drugged up pussy. Fuck that shit for a joke.

My loyalty is to my club and my brothers who stand beside me. Those who follow the same creed I do since we were patched in. We don't follow anybody's rules but our own - we don't hurt women, children, the elderly or animals. We don't deal drugs and we protect our territory. It's that simple.

# Chapter Three

**Harlow**

Since I live in Stockton, we have to catch the ferry boat over to Newcastle. Otherwise, we would have to take two cars. Plus, it's only a five-minute trip across the water compared to a half hour trip all the way in the car. It can be a pain in the ass, but sometimes I prefer it to driving. There's something about the way the small waves crash against the side of the boat which is calming.

"Thank fuck it's one of the rare nights in Autumn when it's actually warm, otherwise we'd be freezing our tits off right now." Tilly speaks as another wave hits the side of the boat and I feel the light spray of cool water coat my skin.

"Couldn't agree more." Callie grips the safety rail on the side of the boat, hanging on for dear life.

"Do you want to go inside?" Ava murmurs to her.

"Nah, I'm good." Callie tries for a reassuring smile, but she can't fool us, we know she's scared to death.

"Seriously guys, I'm fine. We're about to dock anyway." She nods towards the lit-up dock just ahead of us.

"Do we have a game plan?" Holly asks, changing the subject and looking at everyone before her eyes connect with mine.

"Not really," I murmur.

I run everything through my head one more time. Remembering what I know about the month leading up to Julie's murder.

"Run through everything that we know again." Alexis knows exactly what I'm thinking.

Even though they're as aware of everything as I am, they know it helps me process and put everything in line in my head.

"About a month before she died, she got the job of keeping track of the books at *Club Ivy*. I thought it was weird, considering the Deadly Sins MC would have had someone to do that." I shake my head, I'm still confused by it all. Instead of dwelling on it, I move onto my next point. "She met a guy who also worked there, Elliot, and she was really excited when he asked her out. I know I need to find this guy, he may hold the answers we need because if you ask me, he sounded shady as fuck." I grumble the last part to myself, but with Tilly standing so close she hears me and nods her head. She knows exactly what I mean.

"Every time we planned to get together so I could meet him, he always had some bloody excuse as to why he couldn't make it."

"Have you met anyone named Elliot?" Ava asks.

I shake my head. "No, but I've only been there a month and haven't met everyone yet."

"So, let's find this Elliot guy and hopefully he can tell us what we need." Callie takes a few shaky steps towards me and links her arm with mine as the boat docks. I know it's more for her safety since she had to let go of the safety rail.

Making our way onto the platform, Callie lets out a relieved breath. Resting my hand on top of her arm, I give it a light squeeze. She gives me a smile in return and we begin the fifteen-minute walk to the club.

***

Getting to the front door of *Club Ivy* was no easy feat considering the line of people trying to push their way in. Pulling the invitations from Peyton's clutch purse, I flash them at the two burly bouncers standing by the door. They're wearing cuts with patches which state they're Prospects. Nodding, they let us pass. Tonight, isn't invitation only but if you have managed to get your hands on one, you're granted exclusive access over those walking in off the street. Thank fuck I had the common sense to grab seven so we didn't have to wait in the bloody line. Deep down I knew the girls wouldn't let me do this on my own. Smiling as brightly as I can at the bouncers, the girls and I rush into the small alcove where there's a coat check. Two girls stand in front of double frosted glass doors which lead into the main part of the club, handing out wristbands and checking IDs.

"Hey, Chloe." I head towards one of the girls who usually works behind the bar with me.

"Harlow. Oh, my god, look how hot you look!" She gives me a gorgeous smile, making her blue eyes sparkle as blonde curls bounce on her shoulders.

I give her a genuine smile before giving her a quick hug.

"Thanks, these are my friends." I make the quick introductions as the beat behind the doors gets louder.

She hands us all a wristband and we each drop $20 into her hand for our entry fee before making our way towards the heavy glass doors which lead into the main area of the club.

"Be good. Be bad. Pick your flavour," Chloe calls out seductively from behind us as I push the door open. I wave back at her, she wouldn't hear me over the music if I spoke anyway. Looking around, I observe the faux walls they have put up to create separate rooms for each sin around the main dance floor. I must admit everything is pretty over the top, but it looks really good. I weave through the crowd of sweaty dancing bodies as *Jessie's Girl* by *Rick Springfield* blasts from the speakers. I glance over my shoulder at the girls to make sure they're following me as I make a beeline for the bar.

"Fuck me standing and fucking sideways, you have *got* to be fucking kidding me!" Holly grits out.

If we weren't so close, I wouldn't have heard her or even noticed that she'd stopped dead in her tracks. She's staring into the crowd of people on the dance floor. Bobbing my head from left to right, I try to see what has got her so pissed off. That's when I spot the guy Holly has been seeing for the past couple of months grinding up against some bitch. Before I can stop her, she's shoulder barging her way through the crowd. Grabbing Richard by the arm, she swings him around and stands toe to toe with him.

"Fuck!" Peyton shouts as we race to Holly's side.

We're not sure what she'll do and considering we're in a club that has bikers in it, this shit could get ugly real fast. Reaching her side first, I grab her arm but she shakes me off angrily. The air around us becomes thick with tension and I feel all eyes are on us. I glance around frantically and see a huge guy wearing a cut coming down the wooden stairs which lead up to office. He's staring straight at us.

"This isn't good," Tilly murmurs as we watch the guy part the crowd like it's the fucking Red Sea. He's heading directly for us.

"Fuck!" I grit.

"You're a dick-less wonder, you know that Richard?" Holly shouts over the music.

I watch as Richard tries to reach out to touch her. Before he can make contact, she pulls her arm back and punches him square in the face. He stumbles and hits the ground hard, blood pours from his nose. It was that good of a hit, I feel like cheering, until I remember where we are.

"You bitch," he wheezes while holding his nose and groaning in pain.

"Don't you ever come near me again, you dick-less prick!" Holly spits out just as the huge ass biker reaches us.

Looking him up and down, I swallow hard. He's covered in tatts, has short dark hair and he's bloody huge! Not just in width, he's at least six feet two inches. The seven of us are like dwarfs at between five feet and five feet five inches. *We're so fucking screwed.*

"Problem here, woman?" His gruff voice spits out while looking Holly up and down.

Without missing a beat, and not giving a fuck who she's talking to, she bites out, "This dick-less wonder needs a fucking pink skirt!" She's still glaring at so called dick-less as he tries to get to his feet. "Fucken pussy!" Holly spits out before kicking him in the stomach.

"Shit, Holly," I squeak out, not sure of what I should do.

Looking back at the biker, I watch as a smirk twitches at the corner of his lips before he bends down and with one hand, lifts Richard until his feet are dangling off the ground, lifting him like he weighs nothing more than a newspaper.

"Time to leave," he spits into Richards face. "Enjoy your evening, ladies." He nods as he steps past us, still holding an outraged Richard in the air.

My head is absolutely spinning, how the hell did we not get thrown out?

"I need a drink." Holly spins around and heads for the bar.

"How the hell did we manage to not kicked out?" Tilly asks.

I shrug my shoulders, not having a bloody clue.

Leaning against the bar, I study Holly standing next to me as she orders eight shots of Tequila. I must give her a funny look at the number she's ordered and she leans over and whispers into my ear, "I need two after that."

"Are you okay?"

"I will be."

The shots are lined up in front of us and I smile at the guy who served us as Peyton hands over the cash. He must be new, I've never met him before. Either that or we just haven't been on shift together. "Thanks," I yell over the music while grabbing my staff card so we can get a discount.

"No worries." He smiles as his eyes travel down to my tits. I roll my eyes, seriously, every guy is the bloody same.

Turning our backs to the bar, each of us girls brings our shot up. After we all do tops and bottoms with the glasses, we throw the shots back. I hum at the bite in my throat while Ava and Callie wince at the taste, making me laugh.

"Okay ladies, where should we start?" I yell over the music.

"Why don't we check each of the rooms out first?" Peyton eyes the *Greed* room and what looks like a mini casino set up inside. Eyeing each of the rooms, I can't see a lot so, I nod that I'm keen. I keep my eyes peeled for my boss, Trevor. If anybody can lead me to this Elliot guy, it's him.

***

After about two hours of checking everything out, we leave Tilly and a laughing Peyton, in the throws of kicking everyone's ass at Blackjack. We again make our way around the club to see if I can find Trevor, it looks like luck isn't on my side tonight.

"They're playing a good mix tonight and damn these bloody bikers are smoking." Callie giggles as the first bars to *Beautiful Trauma* by *Pink* begins to play.

"Do you wanna dance?" Holly bounces on the balls of her feet like a little kid going into a toy shop for the first time.

Without waiting for an answer, she grabs Callie's and Ava's hands and drags them through the crowd to the dance floor.

"Should we join them?" I ask Alexis.

"Let's go to the ladies' room first."

"Sounds good." I nod and turn before heading in the direction of the front doors where the bathrooms are. Waiting in line, I start to wonder if I will ever get the answers I need.

Maybe coming here tonight wasn't the best way to gather information after all. Feeling a little defeated, I lean against the row of sinks.

"What are you thinking so hard on 99?" Alexis breaks through my thoughts and I try not to laugh at her *Get Smart* reference.

"Just wondering if tonight was worth it." I chew on my bottom lip.

"Well I'm not sure, but I do know this...." She pushes her glasses back up her nose. "....between work and everything else we have going on, we haven't had a night out together for way too long." She pauses for a moment and something crosses her face. I wonder if I'm missing something. "What I mean is - we're all here together so we may as well make the most of it."

"Your right." I shrug. "But, what am I missing here, what do you mean *with everything else going on?*"

"Nothing, just life in general." She answers way too quickly before dashing into the cubicle that just became free.

*There's more than what she's letting on, I feel it deep in my bones.*

I head into the next empty cubicle.

After doing our business, we wash our hands and head back to the main area. Pushing the door open, we have barely gone a few feet when Alexis stops in her tracks.

"Holy hotness, Batman," Alexis breathes under her breath, but as one song morphs into another at the same time, I manage to hear what she's said.

I laugh. I love my nerdy friend and only she would reference a hot guy in that way.

"What? Who? Where?" I fire out while looking around, grabbing her arm and pulling her to the side away from the bathroom door.

"If you shut up for a second, I'll tell you and this isn't one of those times to make it bloody obvious we're looking. Okay?" She flicks her eyes towards me and gives me a pleading look.

Nodding, I make the sign of the cross over my heart and pretend to zip my lips, making her smirk.

"Over by the main doors," she murmurs into my ear while looking over my shoulder.

Swinging around, I get up on my tippy toes and crane my neck to look over a few people who are standing near us and making it hard for me to see. Shooting me a funny look, they walk off and I have the perfect side view of the guy Alexis is talking about.

"For shit's sake, Harlow, could you be any more obvious? Have you even heard the word, subtle?"

Ignoring her grousing at me, I take in the bear of a man because bloody hell, there is no other way to describe him. He kind of looks like Seth Rogen, but with tatts and a scowl. He's tall and stocky with a beard. I notice he's wearing a cut. What is it with all us girls tonight, only zeroing in and crushing on the bikers? Turning back to Alexis, I watch as her eyes take the man in. I bite my lip to stop myself from saying something stupid. I don't want to upset her, I know it took a lot for her to come here tonight, especially wearing what she's wearing. It's not that she's shy, but she is very self-conscious about her body. Not that there's anything wrong with it.

"Why don't you go and say, hello," I encourage her.

Biting her lip, she looks at me and back to the man before peering at the ground. Running her hands down the nightie she's wearing, she shakes her head.

"You're gorgeous, Babe," I say reassuringly.

She looks over at the man again and I can see she is building herself up to go over there, but then something crosses her face.

"I just need a minute," she mumbles before turning and dashing back into the ladies' room.

*What the hell was that about?* I look back to the man, but this time he isn't alone. A beautiful woman is with him, but as she raises an arm to put around him, he grabs it, shakes his head and eyeballs another man. That's when I see Trevor standing in front of him, but before I can approach them, the burly biker grabs him by the shirt, lifts him off his feet, brings him to eye level and sneers into his face. Holy shit, what did my boss do to piss off a biker? Without realising what I'm doing, I start towards them. By the time I push past people who are blocking my way and get to where they were, they're long gone. Shit, where the fuck did they go? I scan the area, but they're nowhere to be seen. Shit, that could have been my only chance. Damn it! Grumbling to myself, I make my way back to the bathrooms and lean against the wall to wait for Alexis.

"This is for all the lover's out there tonight," the DJ announces over the microphone before the first bars of

*H.O.L.Y.* by *Florida Georgia Line* starts to play. I tap my foot to the beat as my eyes search the dance floor for the girls. People start leaving the floor to go to the bar and I notice the girls swinging each other around and laughing. Something about that moment sends warmth radiating through me - knowing no matter what, these girls have my back. No matter the situation. I know I can't bring these girls into this mess and I will do everything in my power to protect them. With that thought settled in my mind, I push from the wall as Alexis appears from the bathroom.

"Let's dance with the girls." I nod towards them and a bright smile graces Alexis lips before she nods.

"Let's do it." She grabs my hand and we make our way over at the same time Peyton and Tilly walk onto the dance floor.

As the lyrics ring out - *I'm high on loving you*, me and the girls do our best to keep up with the song. We fail miserably and crack up laughing when a guy walks over, grabs Holly around the waist and starts to dance with her. Turning, she shakes her head, saying she doesn't want to dance. The guy doesn't take the hint and tries to pull her back into his arms. Before she can push him away again, he hits the floor hard. It's like everything moves in slow motion. The rest of us stop and when we look to Holly's left, we see the burly biker from earlier. The one who tossed Richard out on his ass. He's standing over the guy and looks pissed. I study his cut and notice the numerous patches, but the one that says *Enforcer* stands out over everything else.

"You causing more trouble, Woman?" he gruffs out over the music.

When he looks at Holly, I notice the hard edge to his eyes softens a little. Another guy wearing a similar cut picks the guy up off the floor and I realise it's the one Alexis was eyeing. His patch reads Sgt. At Arms and below it, *Razor*.

"What if I am, Pyro?" Holly cocks her hip, raising her chin in challenge.

I swear to God she has absolutely lost her damn mind.

"I may have to keep an eye you." He folds his arms over his hard chest and stares down at her.

Holy friggin shit, is it just me or did the air in here just get even hotter?

"Don't pretend like you haven't been already, big boy," she purrs out.

"Holly." I grab her arm at the same time the guy drops his arms.

After a few moments where it seems they just stare at each other, a deep rumbling laugh spills from him, causing Holly and the rest of us to crack up.

"You're going to be a handful and I can't wait," he growls before turning and walking away.

I notice the other guy staring hard at Alexis, but she has her head down staring at the floor. "Oi!" I nudge her but she shakes her head. When I look back to the guy, a smirk kisses his lips before he turns and drags the guy who tried to grope Holly towards the front doors.

"I think I need a drink after that!" Peyton shouts and I nod.

Turning, we all make our way to the bar. After grabbing another drink, we head back to the dance floor. After a few songs, we need a break and head towards a high-top table which is vacant. Now is as good a time as any to try and escape without them getting suss.

"I think I'm gonna head home, girls."

"Oh, what, why?" Tilly slurs.

"I'm not feeling one hundred percent." I lie, hoping the girls have had enough to drink to let me slip out alone. "I better try and get some sleep before I have night shift tomorrow night." I glance at my watch, it reads 1am, "I mean tonight," I laugh.

"Wait, we'll come with you." Holly grabs her drink and throws it back.

"How are you going to get home?" Ava asks.

"It's fine, you girls stay and enjoy the rest of the night. I'm just gonna call a cab." Grabbing my phone and keys from Peyton's clutch, I don't give them a chance to argue. I wave over my shoulder and try to blend into the crowd. When I hear them calling my name, I ignore it, feeling guilty as shit for lying. But, tonight I came here to get information and so far, I haven't gotten a fucking thing. I need to see if I can find Trevor again.

***

Stepping from the club into the cool morning air, I rub my arms and make my way towards the cab pickup line. I feel absolutely defeated. I've spent the past half an hour since I left the girls searching for Trevor without any luck.

Needing a smoke, it hits me - I left them in Peyton's clutch.

"Just fucking great," I grumble to myself.

"Hey, you're the new chick." A guy's voice sounds from beside me.

I turn to find it's the sleazy bar tender from earlier. I nod in answer, not in the mood to be hit on.

"I'm L," he introduces himself.

I take in the black shirt and pants the guys have to wear with the Ivy logo on the front, his pale face and red hair.

"Nice to meet, ya."

I notice he's smoking.

Fuck, I really didn't want to talk to this guy, but I need a smoke.

"I'm Harlow, you wouldn't happen to have one of those I can bum off you, would you?" I nod to the smoke in his hand and watch as his eyes light up.

"Sure do, beautiful." He pulls the packet out of his pants pocket and hands me one.

Muttering, thanks, I step out of the line and head towards the carpark so I don't annoy anyone when I light it up. Low and behold, L follows me.

"I've got something harder you can smoke." He steps to my side and rubs his shoulder against mine.

"I'm good, thanks. I don't do drugs," I bite out.

I don't mean to be rude but just the mention of drugs gets my back up.

"Oh beautiful, I didn't mean drugs," he says close to my ear.

His hot, rank breath puffs over my neck, sending disgust running through me.

"Not interested," I manage to say before he yanks my arm hard.

He swings me around and my back hits a concrete wall, I hit my head hard and see stars.

"Fuck!"

"Not yet, beautiful, but soon." He grips my hair hard while his hand slides under my dress.

"Get your fucking hands off me!" I scream. Bringing one hand up, I push against his chest. With my other hand, I try to stop his hand from wandering under my dress. For a small guy, he's fucking strong. Looking into his pale eyes, I notice how blown they are. Fuck, he's high.

"I said, get the fuck off me!" I bring my knee up into his nuts, making him scream out in pain. He drops to his knees but not before he lashes out and hits me straight across the face.

*Fuck, that stung like a bitch.* My eyes become watery and while sucking the pain down, I bring the heel of my boot down on his nuts again.

"Piece of shit," I spit out before hearing the crunch of boots on the gravel road in front of me.

Snapping my eyes up, my breath leaves me in a whoosh when a pair of broad shoulders step into my view. I note the VP patch on his cut and the name, Mercy. I lick my suddenly dry lips when his piercing green eyes lock onto mine.

"Need a lift?" He nods to a sleek black *Harley* that's sitting at the end of a row of bikes.

I suck down a deep breath in an attempt to control myself as his deep gravelly voice sends shivers down my spine. Without saying a word, I look to the bike and back to him. I'm not sure what the hell I'm thinking when I nod and head towards the bike. As I pass, I hear him hiss out a breath, sending delicious tingles directly to my clit.

*Fuck what the hell am I doing?* I ask myself as I throw one leg over the back of his bike.

# Chapter Four

**Drake**

Stepping out into the early morning air, I rub my face. I'm completely fucking done for the night. I've had about enough of this shit for one night and I have to be back in less hours then I care to fucking count. Nodding my head at the two prospects on guard duty at the door, I pull out a smoke and light it. Making my way towards the carpark, I take a deep breath and exhale slowly, watching the white smoke float away.

I hear someone shout, "Fuck!" before what sounds like a low groan off to my right. Snapping my eyes to the side of the carpark that's lined with buildings, I see a man caging a woman in. It's obvious she doesn't want to be there.

*Fucken hell, I'm too tired for this shit tonight.*

I make my way towards them and as I get closer, I hear the woman call out, "I said get the fuck off me!" right before she brings her knee up and slams him square in the balls. I wince knowing that shit would have hurt. A low growl slides up my throat when he raises his hand and smacks her across the face. I'm close enough now to see her eyes glass over. I can't help thinking that any minute now, I'm gonna have to deal with a crying drunk chick and fuck if I was in the fucking mood for this shit tonight. After a few seconds, a look crosses her face and instead of breaking down, she brings her leg up and jams the heel of her boot into his nuts again.

"Piece of shit," she spits out.

I'm fucking gobsmacked. Instead of breaking down, she harnessed all her emotion into one I know so well – Anger.' That right there should have been my first clue to stay the fuck away from her. I should have turned and walked the fuck away, gone back inside. Instead, I find myself asking if she needs a lift. Staring at me, she takes in my cut before flicking her eyes towards my bike. Sliding the tip of her luscious pink tongue across her bottom lip causes my gut to cramp at the motion. I grit my teeth to prevent a groan slipping from my throat. When her eyes turn back to mine, she nods before making her way towards my *Harley*. As she passes, I hiss out a breath when I inhale her delicious vanilla smell. When I look back to the piece of shit still laying on the ground holding his balls in his hands, I chuckle. I knew he was a pussy. Any man who puts his hands on a woman is a gutless little bitch.

"You're lucky she got to you first." I speak menacingly quiet. "L, if that's your name, stay the fuck away from her. Consider yourself warned." I make it clear, I know who the fuck he is.

I whistle to get the prospects attention, call them over and tell them to deal with this piece of shit. Looking towards my bike, I grind my teeth together, wondering how fucking painful this is gonna be to ride with her wrapped around me while the scent of vanilla fills my nose. Fuck she looks good on my bike, and that bloody latex outfit mixed with her smooth skin scattered with ink is not helping the situation one little bit.

As I make my way towards her, the streetlamp bounces off her whiskey brown hair, reminding me of the scotch I was drinking earlier. My semi hard cock punches against the zipper of my pants when I wonder just how sinful she would taste. Or, how she would look riding my hard cock as I spanked her ass for wearing something like this to begin with. Fuck, I know the party was called 7 deadly Sins, but how the fuck can she have me wanting to sin in every fucking way possible just by wearing that outfit? To have her pretty little mouth taking my cock to the back of her throat while those dark eyes stare up at me, begging for more.

Running a hand roughly through my hair then, down the side of my face, I try to erase the images playing on a loop through my head before my semi turns hard as fucking steel.

Fuck, she hasn't said a damn word to me and she already has me wanting everything she has to offer.

"Where to?" I try to control the gruffness in my voice.

"If you could drop me at the ferry dock that would be great, thanks," she breathes out in a smooth smoky breath.

Fuck, it's a voice I could get drunk on. Not trusting my voice to answer, I nod and hand her my helmet. I'm surprised to see she knows how to fasten it. I glance at my watch, it's quarter to two in the morning.

"Doesn't the last ferry leave at midnight?"

"Ah, shit," her face falls. "I forgot." She starts to take off the helmet, but I put my hand out to stop her and she freezes instantly.

"It's all good, just tell me where to go?" I realise I've been instinctively rubbing the side of her face with my thumb, feeling the smoothest skin I have ever felt.

Fuck, get it together. Dropping my hand, I shove both into my pockets and wait for her to answer.

"I can get a cab." She eyes the cab pick-up area across the street.

"Just tell me," I don't mean to snap. I'm exhausted and a little pissed at the thought of her having to pay to go home in a cab when I can take her. A possessiveness I have never felt before slices through me at the thought of the cab driver seeing her in this outfit. Looking back to her eyes, I notice the hard edge to them before she speaks.

"With a fucking tone like that, I don't fucking think so." She climbs off my bike and slams my helmet into my chest.

"Oooff, what the fuck?" I'm completely fucking stunned. No-one has ever spoken to me like that before. If they did, they wouldn't make it two feet, let alone the ten she's covered. "Hey, Lemon Drop," I call out. She swings around. She's pissed. Storming back to me, she points a finger into my chest and pushes. I'm too fucking big for her to make much of an impression. I look down in amusement as her nail digs in.

"What the fuck did you just call me?" she hisses and looks me dead in the eyes.

Even though she barely reaches as high as my chest, this chick has balls. Every second her eyes shoot daggers my way, the more I fucking want her.

"I said, get your ass on the bike."

"No, you called me Lemon Drop, what the hell does that even mean?"

Not bothering to answer, I jam the helmet on her head. She angrily bats my hands away and I chuckle as she fastens it herself.

"What's your name, anyways?" Her eyes are riveted to me.

"Mercy."

She rolls her dark eyes in disgust. "I meant your real name. I'm pretty sure your parents didn't name you *Mercy* at birth."

"If you get your ass on the bike and tell me where you live, I'll consider telling you."

She huffs out another breath before throwing her leg over the bike, folds her arms across her chest and gives up the address.

"It's Drake," I answer as I climb on.

Turning around slightly, I grab her hips and slide her forward so her body is flush against mine. I grit my teeth as the hard on I was fighting hits full force, to the point of pain.

"Fuck," I mumble.

"Everything okay, Drake?"

I lock my eyes with her dark orbs. She's fighting back a smile, knowing full well what she's doing to me. I grunt in response. Turning back around, I start up the bike. As the pipes rumble and echo around us, her hands rest lightly on my waist. Grabbing them, I wrap them around my stomach and her tits push into my back.

"By the way, my name is Harlow," she murmurs seductively into my ear in a voice as smooth as silk. I can't stop the low growl crawling out of my throat as her warm breath runs down my neck. Even her name drips fucking sin. I don't know what the fuck is happening right now, but seriously, fuck me with this shit because when I get her to where she wants to go, she'll be lucky to walk away free.

***

By the time I pull into the kerb in front of what I presume is her place about half an hour later, my cock is as hard as stone and all I want to do is wrap her pussy around it to soothe the ache in my balls. Pushing her hands against my shoulders, she climbs off. After turning my bike off, I wait for her to hand me the helmet before I get off and stretch my legs, re-adjusting my cock.

"What are you doing?" she asks a little breathlessly.

"Walking you to your door." Placing my hand at her lower back, I begin to guide her up the path towards the brick townhouse.

"Thanks for the lift, it's the most fun I've had in a long time."

Sadness coats her words but before I can ask if she's okay, she speaks again.

"Do you want to come in for coffee or something?" She smiles shyly and kicks the toe of her boot against the front step.

Well I'll be fucking damned. I was right when I called her a Lemon Drop. I chuckle.

"What's so funny?"

"I was right when I called you, Lemon drop."

"Shit, I'd forgotten about it. Why did you call me that?" She turns to face me after she opens the front door and I notice a dim glow through the house.

"Because, on the outside you're sour with sass, but if you lick a little longer and reach the centre, you're sweet and soft."

A puzzled look crosses her face before a mischievous smile curves her plump lips.

"You haven't licked anything yet," she winks.

"Oh, I plan to lick, suck, bite until you're screaming my name, Babe, but first you need to know I don't date. I don't do all flowers and shit so, if you want me, this is it, Babe. Take it or leave it. I probably won't even call you tomorrow."

I run a single finger down her temple, across her cheek and across her bottom lip before pulling back and dropping my hand to my side.

"Who said I wanted you to call me?" She licks her lips and hums as she begins pulling me inside by the shirt.

"Right fucking answer," I growl. Gripping her around the waist, I crush my mouth against hers, taking what I want. When I lift her off the ground, she wraps her legs tight around my waist and I feel the heat of her pussy through the thick denim of my jeans. Gripping her ass with one hand, I squeeze and grab layers of her rich whiskey coloured hair in a fist at the top off her head. She groans into the kiss before she pulls back panting, arching her neck. Gripping a bit harder, I pull her head back further, exposing her slender neck even more. I slide my mouth down her neck, grazing my teeth as I go and moan as the taste of vanilla coats my tongue.

"Fuck, Babe." I slam us both into the entry wall.

"Don't stop," she says on a smoky whisper, skyrocketing my need for her.

"Not on your fucking life," I grit out.

Leaning back a little, I let the wall take her weight. Bringing my hand up, I rip down the front of her dress, exposing her pierced nipples. Her phone tumbles onto the carpeted floor.

"Fuck," I grunt.

I latch onto the first nipple and she arches her back, pushing her tit further into my mouth. Moving to the other one, I give it the same treatment. Whimpers leave her sexy mouth as I run my teeth around the metal ring.

"You like that?"

Before she can answer, I grip the ring with my teeth and give it a light tug.

"Fuck," she groans while tightening her legs around my waist.

She circles her still covered pussy over the front of my jeans. Gritting my teeth against the need to come, I reach down with both hands and rip the remaining part of her dress clean off.

I watch as she lifts her hands and starts pulling on the piercings, growling at the sight. Without giving her any warning, I grab the sides of her panties, ripping them so they fall to the floor with her dress. Moving my hands to her ass again, I squeeze. Tearing the fishnet stocking down the middle, I pull them from her body. She slides her hands down my chest before running them up my cut to my shoulders. Normally I wouldn't let anyone touch my cut, but I'm curious to see what she'll do.

Locking my eyes with hers, I watch them soften as she slowly peels the cut down my arms. She folds it neatly and bending to one side a little, places it on a side table I didn't know was there. The way she treats it so reverently makes me realise, she knows what it means to me. After a moment, the softness disappears from her eyes and is replaced with fire. She rips my shirt over my head before lowering her hands to my belt and snapping it open. Closing my eyes, I savor the feel of her soft hand as it wraps around my hard cock. I hiss and snap my eyes open when I feel her teeth on my collarbone.

"You still with me?" she purrs.

Releasing my grip on one ass cheek, I grab a condom from my pocket. Bringing it to my teeth, I rip the packet open. Harlow takes it from me and with one hand still steadily stroking my cock, she smears leaking pre-cum around the tip. I groan, letting my head roll back on my shoulders. She lowers her other hand and rolls the condom on before twisting her fingers into my hair, tugging a little on the ends. She rubs the head of my cock against her clit. Her breathing picks up and arching her back at the sensation, she rubs her tits against my bare chest. I'm done with this teasing bullshit.

"Fuck, Harlow, ride me, Babe." I groan when the tip of my cock runs over her clit again.

Grabbing her ass and pulling her lower half forward until the back of her shoulders rest against the wall, I bury my face in her gorgeous tits. On the next down motion, I push forward, she rocks down and takes me inside her tight fucking pussy.

"Shit. Shit. Shit" I grit out between clenched teeth as she starts to move against me.

I grip her harder and know she'll have bruises on her ass tomorrow, but fuck, if it isn't the best fucking feeling in the world. The possessive feeling from before grips me at the thought of her having marks left by me.

"Oh God," she gasps.

"Fuck that, Babe. Say my fucking name when I'm deep inside you." I grunt and push the rest of the way inside, feeling her pussy walls tense around me.

"Drake, fuck," she calls out before slamming her mouth against mine.

Lifting my hand to her hair, I grip a handful and take control. My tongue slides across hers, tasting every whimper as they escape her throat. Moving her head to the side, I devour every inch of her mouth, taking what's mine as I slam into her over and over, feeling her pussy clench, tightening around my cock each time I pull back. Pulling my mouth away from hers, I slide my tongue across the jawline to her ear before nipping the lobe, making her hiss. She meets me thrust for thrust, and I suck the lobe into my mouth to soothe the sting.

"You have a greedy pussy, Babe," I growl into her ear.

Her breaths are short pants and sweat soaks our skin.

"Fuck," she spits out. The heel of her boots dig into my ass, pushing me deeper.

"Drake!" she screams out.

I feel her warm cum all over my cock and opening my mouth, I latch onto her collarbone and bite down. An electric current charges down my back. My balls draw up and I explode inside her. All the while, running through my head is the fact she is never getting free from me now.

Yep, I'm fucked. I never asked for this. I never wanted this. But now that I have it, I'm never letting her go. Yep, I'm definitely fucked.

# Chapter Five

**Harlow**

"What the hell did I do?" I mumble under my breath so as not to wake the hulk of a man sleeping next to me. Peeking over my shoulder, I lie as still as possible and take in his features which aren't as hard as I remember from last night. My fingers twitch, wanting to run through his five o'clock shadow on his firm jaw. I double check he's still sleeping and recall the piercing cool blue colour of his eyes, the way they seemed to lock onto every move I made. My eyes travel down to his plump lips and I suck my bottom lip into my mouth as I remember his taste of cinnamon and a touch of scotch. Releasing a soft hum, my eyes close and flashes of the way his rough hands worked their way around my body fill my head.

Possession and dominance radiated from every touch, sending electricity running through my veins. Causing the cells in my body to release small electric shocks to each of my muscles, ensuring they were awake and not missing a single thing. Squeezing my thighs together, I struggle to control the pulse in my clit as his hand cups my pussy. Turning my face back to the bedside table, I try to calm the pitter patter of my heart as it races, caused by staring at this man. *I cannot fall for this guy,* I repeat over and over in my head. I hope the words catch up to my heart because something deep inside me is telling me it's already too late. Letting out a soft groan, I rub the sleep from eyes. Last night was a total bust. I went to Club Ivy to get answers and ended up sleeping with a biker. And, not just any biker. No, I slept with the motherfucking Vice President of the club, a man who could have been involved in Julie's death. Sucking down the lump which has formed in my throat, I close my eyes as they glass over and take a few deeps breaths when I feel my control slipping.

"I will not cry," I chant to myself on a whisper over and over again.

I squeeze my eyes tight when I feel the hand resting on my boob flex making my body hum and my clit pulse harder.

Fuck, I need him to leave. The way he's holding my body so possessively, as if someone is going to take me away at any minute, has my already messed up heart screaming for him to be mine. I know it's impossible, he made his feelings quite clear and I felt the same. I have no time for a man in my life, especially not this man. So, why the hell does it hurt so much to think of him walking out the door and never coming back. What if he already has somebody in his life who keeps his bed warm, fulfills his needs? Jealousy, like I've never felt before, rushes through my veins like hot lava. I know I need him to leave, for the first time in a long time he made me feel safe, protected. I never wanted the feeling to end, but I knew this was a onetime thing. As I'm about to roll over, he pulls me closer. His barrel chest seems to envelope my back. A sleepy groan washes down my neck, sending goosebumps breaking out over my skin. Biting my lip, I catch the whimper that wants to escape as one of his thick fingers runs small circles around my now throbbing clit. My toes curl at the sensation of the slightest touch, my body becomes rigid and a fast and hard orgasm slams into me, knocking the breath from my lungs.

"Morning, Babe."

His voice, laden with sleep, has to be the sexiest sound I've ever heard. I know I need to get up and put as much distance as I can between us. Taking a few extra seconds to relish the feel of him, I grit my teeth and slide out of his hold, taking the bedsheet with me.

"I need the bathroom." I put as much strength as I can muster into my words so he gets the hint. "Thanks for last night, I guess I'll see you around," I say over my shoulder. My eyes flick over his muscled, tattooed naked body and I curse myself for looking. His body is carved from sin and I bring the sheet to my lips to make sure I'm not drooling from one simple look.

"See you around?" His question comes out on a grunt.

Snapping my eyes to his, I notice the blue of his eyes is sharp, like a piece of ice. It sends shivers down my spine. He pushes to his feet and stands to his full height. I battle to keep my focus on his eyes and not his naked body as he closes the distance between us. Instinctively, I retreat until my back hits the wall. I should feel scared when his massive body cages me in, but my body betrays me and begins to hum. Reaching up, I place my hands against his hard chest, the hair tickles the palms of my hands. He leans down, so he's at eye level with me. I jut my chin up so he knows I'm not scared of him. A smirk kisses the side of his mouth.

"No escaping me now, Lemon Drop." His voice is husky sending tingles through every cell.

"One time... One night... That's it... No more," I mumble. "That's what you said." I need my mouth to catch up to my words as they tumble out of me. I need to speak in full sentences, but with him so close and his warm breath rushing over my skin, nothing is making sense.

"I changed my mind."

His words confuse me. I'm not sure what the hell he means, but before I get a chance to say anything, his mouth crashes down against mine, preventing any more words from spilling free. I freeze, not sure what the fuck is happening.

"Fucking, kiss me." He grunts into my mouth after a moment.

It snaps my mind to what is happening and grabbing him by the hair, I push my tongue against his and fight for control. His teeth nip my tongue causing me to moan and surrender. One hand lands on my ass, the other twists in my hair, tugging the strands and causing me to arch my neck. He angles my head to delve deeper, sending sparks of electricity shooting through me once again. Grunting, he lifts me and slams my back against the wall, photo frames hanging there, shake.

"Fuck." He pulls back, sucking in air.

He sounds like he's just run a marathon. I raise fingertips to touch my tingling lips, trying to catch my breath.

"This *isn't* over!"

"But..." It's all I manage to say before he pulls on my hair, sending delicious tingles racing down my spine.

"Lemon Drop, this shit is far from over."

There is so much possessiveness coating his words, all I can do is nod. I know if I did try to speak at this moment, nothing would come out anyways. His hard cock rests against my now throbbing clit and I move my lower half, trying to get friction. To take what I want. Words and thoughts from earlier float away and I'm left in a bubble of need that only this man can fix.

"Fuck," he growls before his teeth latch onto my bottom lip.

He sucks it into his warm mouth, my fingers twist and pull at his hair, making him grunt.

He pulls back from the kiss and whispers in my ear. "You want this, Babe?"

Moving my hips again, I moan when I feel the hard head of his cock hit my clit. I hiss as a sting crosses my ass and I find my voice.

"Fuck, yes," I whimper as his fingers make contact with my pierced nipple.

I groan as he enters me in one smooth, hard stroke causing me to arch my back. Digging my nails into hard muscle in his back, he moves into my touch on a hiss and strokes harder. Releasing my hair, he grips my hips hard and I know I'll have more bruises to add to the collection from earlier this morning and a thrill runs through me at the thought.

"Every time, Babe."

He slams into me. I don't know what the hell he means by that and right now, I don't give a shit.

"Harder," I moan.

I scrape my nails down his back and leaning forward, I latch onto his collarbone with my teeth, tasting the sweat coating his skin. He turns us around and I grip him tighter now I don't have the support of the wall. He drops me to the bed and pulling out, flips me over onto my stomach. Before I can complain about the loss, he's balls deep inside me again. Deeper this time.

"Fucking, so deep," he groans.

I grunt, not even sure I can say my own name right now. I feel the sting on my ass again, not once but three times, it pushes me higher and I slam back into him, trying to take everything he has to give. Gripping my hips, his fingers bite into my skin. The pain magnifies the euphoria I'm feeling. Feeling his teeth, tongue and lips across my back, sends goosebumps racing over my skin.

"Greedy pussy," he breathes out.

I'm so lost in the feel of him but the swipe with his finger across my back hole makes me jump.

"Easy, Lemon Drop." He runs his finger in circles over my hole, trying to make me relax. "This will be mine soon, too." He pushes in a little, making me gasp at the new sensation and also at the words he says.

"Yours?" I managed to get out, I'm completely fucking confused now.

"Mine," he grits out before slamming into me hard one last time.

My world turns into a kaleidoscope of colours and his deep groans bounce off the walls around me.

"We're far from done."

"But you said…" I breath out, trying to catch my breath.

He rolls to the side, taking me with him so I'm lying on his chest, gasping. I feel his warm release run down my leg.

"Shit!"

"What?" he asks, sounding more awake now.

"You didn't wear a condom." Worry and anger at myself for letting it happen, coats my words.

"Are you mine?"

Pushing out of his hold I snap my eyes to his. "I'm not anybody's!"

He shakes his head and smirks. "That's where you're wrong."

Pushing to my feet, I pace in front of my bed, wondering what the hell is going on.

"Last night you said this was a onetime deal, that you wouldn't call and this...." I wave my hand back and forth between us. ".....wasn't what you had to give."

He sits up in bed and runs a hand through his hair. A frustrated, hard look crosses his face. It reminds me, he's a biker not to be fucked with.

"I never wanted this, but shit happens and now, you *are* mine." He stares straight into my eyes as he speaks.

My body shakes but not from fear. It's something else. I don't know the name for it and for the first time in a long time, I don't know what to say. This is all happening way too fast.

My eyes study the floor. "I'm not your property. You can't just claim me after one night of hot sex and that's all it was."

I want everything he's saying to be true, but we're from two completely different worlds. I need to find who murdered my sister and if his club had anything to do with it, there's no way I can be with a man like him.

"Whether you want to accept it or not, this *is* happening." He climbs to his feet and pulls on his worn blue jeans before padding towards me. He pushes me into the wall again. I turn my face away, not wanting to see how hard and determined his eyes are. Closing my eyes tight I take in a few deep breaths.

"Babe," he whispers against my cheek. He slowly turns my face to his while one hand cups my pussy. "You're mine and so is this." He squeezes me between my legs and my eyes fly open.

I stare into his eyes, they hold so many emotions as they devour every curve of my face.

"But," I whisper.

"But nothing, Babe." He brushes his lips over mine. "Everything about you is mine, from your dark hair to the sexy as fuck tattoos covering your skin. You belong to me in every way. You can keep telling yourself you don't want this, but I can see in your eyes, that it's a lie."

He doesn't give me a chance to speak before his mouth hits mine again in a crushing kiss, my body melts into his. When he tears his mouth from mine, I try to suck in as much oxygen as I can to calm my racing heart as the truth in his words soak through me.

"I have club shit to do but, Babe come this arvo, your ass is mine." He pushes away from me, grabs his shirt off the floor and strides from the room.

Shit, why the hell do his words warm me inside? The idea of belonging to this beast of a man makes my heart pound faster and my head swim with the possibilities.

"Shit." I shake my head.

I need to get my head out of the clouds, forget about the what ifs and concentrate on what needs to be done. Rushing into the bathroom, I make quick work of getting cleaned while planning my next move. Maybe if I head into the club, I'll catch Trevor going over everything from last night. With the decision settled in my mind, I race back to my bedroom and dress in a pair on dark blue jeans and black singlet shirt with *The Ivy* embroidered on the front. After throwing my hair up into a messy bun, I head to the living room and grab my bag, keys and phone. As I reach for the door, someone knocks. Looking at the clock, I see it's only 9am. Considering I've only had around four hours sleep, maybe less, I know I'll have to stop for coffee on the way so it might as well be with whoever is on the other side of the door. Pulling it open, I smile when I see Alexis standing there wearing her work out gear and holding two travel cups of coffee.

"Morning, sweetcheeks."

"Morning." She notices my bag, the way I'm dressed and looks back at me with a puzzled look.

"I need to head into work and see if I can catch Trevor, wanna come?"

"Why not," she shrugs.

"Okay, let's go." I lock up, take the coffee she hands me and we make our way towards my car.

# Chapter Six

**Drake**

Rolling a pen over my knuckles, I lean back in my chair in the office of *Club Ivy* and watch Crank type some shit on the computer in front of him. Looking around, I take in numerous coffee cups lining the desk.

"Been here all night," Shadow says in way of explanation to my raised eyebrows. He's leaning against the wall opposite.

"Just about done," Crank sighs tiredly.

We all ignore the muffled noises coming from Trevor who is tied to a chair in the corner and gagged. "Why the fuck is this taking so long?" I'm pissed I had to leave Harlow to deal with this shit.

"Because this piece of shit hasn't only stolen from the charity and the club, he's also been working against us," Shadow says darkly. He stares at Trevor and plays with a flip knife that he always carries with him.

"What the fuck are you talking about?" I throw the pen back on the desk and push to my feet.

"This piece of shit thought he could throw us under the bus with the *Talon MC*," Shadow growls, hatred laces his words.

"He fucking what?" I look towards him in the corner, pure hatred runs through my blood.

I pace the floor in an attempt to calm myself before I kill this prick with my bare hands.

"Prez stopped in after you left earlier to give us the news and tied Trevor's ass up. He's working out a safe place to deal with him and said he'll call you today." Crank hits a few more keys on the computer in front of him before sighing in satisfaction.

"Reaper was here?" That piece of news surprises me, his cousin must have picked up her kid.

"Yeah, he wasn't here for long, something about his nephew wearing him out." Shadow laughs making me chuckle.

"Found it!" Crank says excitedly at the same moment my phone rings.

I pull it from my pocket to see it's Prez.

"Prez."

"Mercy, brother. I've been in talks with the Grasso family."

"What the fuck for, we don't need the fucking mafia up in our business," I growl.

"Shut the fuck up," Reaper spits out before continuing. "Antonio called us, apparently one of their men killed Ace from the *Talon's MC*."

I smile at the thought that Ace is dead. He was a piece of shit and thought the world owed him everything.

"So, we got to talking and Dominic wants a meeting with us. He has a deal we may be interested in. I agreed."

"What the fuck?" I growl again.

"Just fucking listen." He blows out a frustrated breath and I shut my mouth.

"Since the *Talons* burned down our warehouse where we dealt with our shit, it's only left *Club Ivy*. I don't want shit happening there. Antonio offered up the docks."

I've heard about Antonio's play room before and as much as I don't want to be involved in their mob bullshit, the idea of checking out what Antonio has going, intrigues me.

"Fine," I grunt and listen while he rattles out where we need to take Trevor.

"Right, I'll deal with this shit and meet you back at the clubhouse," I say into the phone.

A female's laugh comes down the line and I hear Prez hiss before he gives a long, drawn out groan. "Fuck," he grunts.

"Reaper?" I wonder what the fuck is happening.

"Talk later."

With those words, he hangs up.

"What the fuck is going on?" Shadow asks.

Crank looks up and turns the computer screen towards me. I lean forward, trying to understand what he's trying to show me. As my eyes scan the screen, I take in all the information Trevor emailed to *Monster*, the VP of the *Talon MC*. I feel the blood heat in my veins when I see the times and places we have scheduled for our next run to Sydney on the screen.

"Piece of shit!" I blow out a hard breath. "We're heading to the docks, boys." I glare at Trevor; a sinister smile pulls at my lips.

***

Pulling my bike up to the docks, I observe a black *Lexus* with tinted windows parked near the side door of the warehouse. Crank pulls up beside me on his bike at the same time Shadow parks the cage with Trevor tied up in the back. Kicking the stand down, I dismount and make my way towards the *Lexus*. My heavy boots crunch against the gravel road. Crank is at my back and we come to a stop a few feet away. The front passenger door opens and a dark-haired man, wearing a suit, steps out. He stands about the same height as me and what skin I do see is covered in tattoos. This must be Antonio, Prez said he was meeting us here.

"Antonio?" I ask raising a brow.

"Si," he nods. "That's Sergio." He nods towards the other guy who's exited the driver's side.

Lifting my chin in hello, I wonder if they know who I am.

"You must be Mercy." Antonio steps towards me and puts out his hand.

Looking down I contemplate whether I should shake it.

"Yep." I shake his hand.

"I don't give a fuck about what shit you need to do, but let's make this quick."

It's all he says and I notice Sergio is looking less then fucking pleased to be here.

"Shadow!" I call.

I turn to see him dragging a kicking Trevor towards the door of the building. Following, we all make our way to the door and head inside before moving towards a lit room at the back.

"Shut the fuck up!" Shadow is losing patience.

He shoves Trevor into a wooden chair next to a long wooden table with straps attached to it.

"Nice set up," I say, looking around.

"Fuck, don't I know it," Antonio chuckles. "Glad you're impressed, now let's get this shit done."

"You can leave," I tell him.

"Not happening." This comes from Sergio.

Shrugging and biting off my anger, I concentrate on the bench which is covered in an assortment of *tools*. Pyro and Razor burst into the room followed by two other guys I don't recognise.

"What the fuck, who the fuck are they?" I glare at Antonio, wondering what the hell is going on.

"Don't take offense, but I don't trust you as far as I can throw you." He points to the two men in suits who have joined us. "That's Nico and Demetri"

"Now all the introductions are done and you've finished comparing dicks, how about we get this shit done?" Crank has a shit eating grin on his face.

Nodding, I grab a curved knife from the table. "Razor, put that piece of shit on the table."

He heads towards a shaking Trevor and some of Antonio's boys walk over to help tie him down. I may not have liked the idea of having these pricks in our business, but I can't help but think this may end better than I thought.

"Trevor, you fucked up big time." I hold the knife up to the light and watch as the rays bounce off the sharp edge.

"Impressive," I murmur and I hear Antonio chuckle.

Moving to the table, I run the knife down the middle of his shirt and pants. It slices them open as if they were paper.

"Trevor, did you piss yourself?" I chuckle when I smell urine.

"Sergio....." Antonio speaks quietly.

I watch as Sergio grabs a bottle of something and walks over to the table. Stepping back, I watch as he pours something strong smelling over Trevor.

"What the fuck was that?"

"Pure alcohol." Antonio shrugs. "It's not the first time someone's pissed themselves and I'd rather smell that than him. An added bonus is, when you slice his skin, it's gonna burn like a bitch."

Looking Antonio dead in the eyes, I see the laughter lying in them and I can't help but chuckle. Yep, this new relationship may just work out.

"Now, where were we?" I look back at Trevor, his eyes are wide with pure terror and he's shaking his head, unable to scream thanks to the gag stuffed into his mouth. Running the tip of the blade against his puny chest, I watch the first drops of blood form and slide down his sides. My head snaps up when I hear the last voice I expected to hear in this place.

"STOP!" Harlow screams.

She's panting like she just ran a mile and my hand freezes with the knife in mid-air. Shadow and Nico each grab one of her arms, stopping her from coming closer to the table. A possessiveness grips me at the sight of them touching what's mine.

"Get your fucking hands off my woman," I snarl.

Shadows eyes widen and he releases her straight away. Nico looks towards Antonio.

"I said let her go, NOW!" My voice is deathly low.

"Nico," Antonio says and the man drops his hands.

Taking a few deep breaths, I try to get myself under control.

"Babe, what are you doing here?" I notice her eyes are glassy as if she's been crying. I look to the piece of shit on the table, wondering if she has feelings for him.

"Does this piece of shit mean something to you?" I ask, not taking my eyes off him. I'm ready to cut his throat. I don't hear her move closer, but I feel her body heat press against my back as she runs her hand down my arm. She reaches for the knife in my hand and I grip it harder.

"Drake," she whispers so only I hear her.

I grunt in response, not knowing what the fuck she's talking about.

"I need answers," she whispers.

My eyebrows pull together, still wondering what the hell she means.

"If I'm yours, trust me." The pleading in her voice squeezes something inside me and I nod, release the knife to her and step back.

Gripping the knife in her hand, she steps forward, leans up on her toes and brushes her lips across mine. "Thank you," she whispers before turning and running the blade down the centre of Trevor's chest. Blood pools on his body. I can't pull my eyes away; this woman blows my goddamn mind. *She* is my *Sin.* I felt it this morning and this moment is setting it in stone.

# Chapter Seven

**Harlow**

"What the fuck are we doing?" Alexis hisses out as we crouch out of sight behind a bunch of oil drums which line the outskirts of Newcastle docks.

"Shhh." I peek over the drums when I hear the echo of bikes slowing down to park.

I look in the direction where a black car with tinted windows is parked and hope this isn't a pass off.

"I told you - when I went upstairs to the office at the club, I overheard Drake say they were bringing Trevor here," I hiss.

"And tell me again how you know this Drake guy?" I can hear the smile in her voice and groan.

I just can't keep my stupid, big, bloody mouth shut, I had to tell her everything that happened after I left them last night. Peeking back over the barrels, I watch as car doors open and two men in suits step out. They look as scary as fuck as they stand talking with Drake while one of the bikers drags a kicking Trevor towards the side of the building.

"Shit." I duck down.

"What?" Alexis whispers.

"We're going to have to go in there," I groan, wondering how far we'll get before someone spots us.

"Um - no way, José." She shakes her head violently. "Are you telling me, you want to go into a big ass building with guys in suits and a bunch of bikers, oh and not just any bikers mind you, they're bloody 1%er's. Have you lost your fucking mind?"

"I have to, Alexis. I need to do this. Trevor is the only lead I have, the only one who might know who killed Julie." I plead for her to understand as my eyes begin to glass over.

"Shit! Shit! Shit!" she curses.

Tears I can't control slide down my cheek.

"Okay," she breathes out. "If we take this nice and slow we might get in there without anyone seeing us." She pokes her head up above the drums before scanning the area and dropping back down. "There are a fair number of pallets stacked around and a forklift. I think if we go that way...." she points over my shoulder. "....we stay behind everything and stay low, we should be alright."

Nodding, I give her a quick hug, wipe my tears away and we creep in the direction she pointed. We stay low and hide behind a stack of pallets when four other guys turn up and make their way inside.

"That was close," Alexis whispers while tugging on my shirt to get my attention.

I nod in agreement before we make a run for the forklift which is near the door we need to enter through.

"Ready?" I breath out.

"Not really." She pushes her glasses up her nose and rubs her hands against her pants.

"Thank you," I whisper. I know once we walk through that door, no matter what happens, she has my back.

"Always, now let's do this before I piss myself."

I giggle before leaning to one side and peering around the forklift, making sure nobody else is around. With the area clear, we dash to the large metal door. I open it as quietly as possible and we slide inside.  The warehouse is dark but we're guided by the light from a back room and make our way to the door. I poke my head around the door, the men's backs are to me and their sole focus is on Trevor. He's lying on a table in the middle of the room and I watch as Drake slides a knife down his chest. Fear slams into me. Fear that I won't get the answers I so desperately need before Drake kills him. It sets my body in motion and I rush into the room.

"STOP!" I scream.

Large hands grip both my arms. Drakes head snaps up and his hand freezes on the knife. A deep growl rumbles in his chest when his eyes lock on the two men holding me. He stares at me and I see his eyes soften a little, my stomach twists at his next words and my heart skips a beat.

"Get your fucking hands off my woman," he snarls between clenched teeth.

One set of hands release me as if I burned him.

"I said let her go, NOW!" His voice is deathly low and clipped.

It sends shivers straight through me and I'm surprised when it travels straight to my clit. Damn this man and my traitorous body.

"Nico." A man's deep voice penetrates my lust filled head and the other guy drops his hands.

I watch as Drake takes a few deep breaths to get himself under control.

"Babe, what are you doing here?" His voice is deep and husky, like he's struggling for control.

His eyes flick back to Trevor and a look crosses his face that I don't understand.

"Does this piece of shit mean something to you?" he asks without taking his eyes off him.

He's jealous! That's what that look is. Knowing this beast of a man is ready to kill at the thought I could have feelings for the weasel of a man, warms me inside. Moving slowly, I block everyone else in the room out and concentrate on the man who just declared to his friends that I'm his. My body presses against his. I slide my hand down his strong, inked, arm until I reach his hand with the knife in it. He grips it harder.

"Drake," I whisper so only he will hear me.

He grunts in response.

"I need answers," I whisper again.

Thick emotion is clear in my words, his eyebrows pull together in confusion.

"If I'm yours, trust me," I plead.

After a few seconds, he nods, releases the knife and takes a step back. Gripping the knife in my hand, I step into his space. I feel the heat and aggression radiating off him in waves and I let it consume me. Leaning up on the tips of my toes, I brush my lips across his and on a whisper, I thank him. Closing my eyes, I taste the hint of cinnamon and a small hum escapes my lips. A soft rumbled growl leaves his throat. Snapping my eyes to his, I see the fire there and I have to turn away before I lose control.

Turning towards the table, I watch for a moment as Trevor's beady little eyes plead with me to set him free. But, I feel nothing. I knew the minute I meet this man he was a weasel. I run the blade down his chest and blood pools around his body. I can't pull my eyes away as crimson drops hit the concrete floor.

"Who is Elliot?" I snarl.

Glancing up when he begins to thrash, I notice he's gagged.

"Demetri." It's the same deep voice I heard earlier.

I raise my eyes to him, he chuckles and winks at me. I feel my cheeks heat but allow my eyes to take in the deathly dark suit and the tattoos which peek out at the cuffs. I bite my lip when I return my eyes to his.

"Damn," I gasp and I hear Alexis giggle.

My head snaps around to where she's standing with a biker beside her, the same one from last night. Bending over, he whispers something in her ear and I notice the blush that creeps over her ivory skin before she ducks her head.

"Antonio..." Drake growls from behind me.

From the corner of my eye, I see Antonio hold his hands up and he has a smirk on his handsome face.

"Trust me, Drake, I'm not interested in your woman. I have one of my own I can barely handle. The fire inside yours reminds me of my Kitten." He chuckles and the other men in suits laugh along with him.

"Thanks, I think," I smile.

"Trust me, it's a compliment, ma'am." Antonio nods to me before his eyes flick back to Trevor on the table.

I turn back to Trevor and realise the guy Antonio called out to has removed the gag from his mouth.

"Who is Elliot?" I run the tip of the knife down his thigh before digging it in and splitting the skin. He lets out a scream.

"I'd answer a bit quicker, if I was you," Drake calls over his screams.

Sucking down deep breaths, Trevor gets his words out on a grunt when I push against the wound with my finger. "He... He works behind the bar at the club."

"I haven't met anyone named Elliot," I mutter more to myself while running through who I've met since I started at the club.

"Why the fuck would you have met them?" Drake demands to know.

I turn my face to his. "Because I work for this piece of shit." I turn around further so he can see my shirt.

"Shit, how didn't I know that?" he mumbles to himself before waving his hand back to Trevor.

"He goes by L," he gasps.

I run the knife back up his stomach and when the name registers in my head, my movement freezes.

"The pussy bartender from last night," Drake says after a few minutes of silence.

"I need to know where he is," I say desperately while turning to Drake.

"Shadow, find Joel and Pete, they dealt with him after my woman beat the shit out of him last night." I try not to smile when I hear the men in the room laugh at Drake's words.

"Yep, she's like my Kitten," Antonio laughs.

"Babe, we're going to finish this piece of shit off then you and me are going to talk about why you need to see this Elliot guy and how the hell you found us here in the first place." Drake steps close enough that his chest rubs against mine and causes my nipples to harden. Gazing into his blue eyes, I see the control he's trying to harness and nod my head.

"Oh shit," I gasp.

I look around frantically, remembering Alexis is still here. I worry about the way she might be handling all this. Over the other side of the table, I notice her head is down and she's still standing next to the biker from last night. Shit, I really need to learn these guys names if I'm gonna be around Drake. I shake the thought off and notice how the man is staring at the top of her head, it's not hard, considering he towers over her.

"Alexis," I say quietly.

She lifts her head and locks her eyes with mine. I'm worried she'll be upset with what's going on.

"I'm okay. Obviously, this piece of shit has pissed somebody off and I'm just glad you know who Elliot is now." I see it in her eyes, she really is okay with this.

***

"Are you sure you're okay?" I ask Alexis as we wait outside the warehouse.

We're waiting with bikers, Razor and Crank and one of the men in a suit. I think he said his name was Nico. As soon as we walked outside, he put his jacket in the car and rolled up his sleeves, he looks like he could bust out of his shirt at any minute.

"Yeah." She doesn't say anything else as she kicks the toe of her *Converse* against the gravel.

"How long do we have to wait?" I ask Razor who is leaning against the side of the building.

"As long as it takes." He shrugs his shoulders and looks towards Crank who is smiling his ass off.

I can't help but laugh, he's kept his mouth shut since Razor told him to shut it or he would cop a boot to it.

"Do you think Drake is pissed we followed him here?" I ask Alexis and watch as a smile curls her mouth.

"Why do you care?" she throws back.

She's right to ask the question. I've never cared if I get in shit for stuff, I'm my own woman and I do what I want. But something about pissing Drake off is equal parts worrying while the other part has tingles running through my body at the thought of the punishment I could get.

"I'm guessing by the look on your face, you're not too worried about it," she laughs.

She laughs so hard that she snorts, cracking me up. Her eyes widen when she realises what she's done and she shies her face away so nobody sees her blush.

"My woman does that too when she laughs," Nico chuckles.

The guy is huge and kind of intriguing, especially that thick accent of his. Actually, now I come to think of it, all the guys in suits have the same accent.

"Nico, was it?" I ask.

He nods.

"I love your accent, where are you from?"

"Jesus, Harlow, are you flirting with him," Alexis grumbles.

I shake my head desperately. Fuck no! First off, he just said he has a missus and secondly, I have a man beast who is beating his chest every five minutes over me. I definitely don't need another one.

"I swear I wasn't chatting you up," I rush out so he doesn't think I'm some lush bouncing around every guy I meet.

"I didn't think you were," he reassures me. "And, I'm Italian." He folds his arms over his broad chest and I see a huge tattoo on the side of his forearm which reads, Josie. There's another name underneath, it's smaller and I can't read it.

"Who's, Josie?" Curiosity gets the better of me.

Chuckling, he stretches out his arm and stares at it for a few minutes.

"Josie is my Petal, the woman of my dreams."

"So, your wife?"

"Si, soon to be anyways," he nods and smiles.

"Any kids?"

"Jesus, Harlow, do you want him to tell you his life story or something?" Alexis asks.

Razor and Crank crack up laughing.

"What? I'm naturally a curious person and since we can't go anywhere, and those two...." I point at the pair of bikers. ".... just grunt when you ask them shit, who else can I suss out?"

Everyone cracks up at that, even me. I shrug my shoulders and wait for Nico to answer.

"Si, we have a little boy," he nods.

"Awesome, what do you do for a living? I know it's some shady shit, but after today I'm kind of shady now, too."

Nico laughs again.

"Fuck, I can't wait to tell my woman about you. Antonio was right, you're exactly like his Missus."

He laughs, but before I can say anything else, the metal door opens and the rest of the rat pack walks out.

"Razor, has Shadow got the information we need?" Drake barks out.

"Yep he's at *Club Ivy* with that Elliot guy now."

I narrow my eyes at Razor, irritated he didn't say anything to me earlier.

"Well, let's get this shit done." Drake strides over, grabs my hand and starts pulling me towards his bike.

"What about Alexis and my car?"

He stops and turns towards Razor; a silent conversation appears to take place before he starts pulling me again.

"Sorted, Babe, now get your sweet ass on my bike before I bend you over it and spank your ass in front of everyone."

He finishes just as Alexis calls out that she'll follow in my car. Turning, I see her almost at my car with Razor hot on her heels.

"Fine," I grumble. I'm pissed Drake thinks he can order me around.

"Lemon Drop, I'm really doing my best to control myself right now so, let's get this shit done. We need to talk." He speaks low so only I hear.

I nod, not wanting to push him too much, but needing him to know I have a voice too. Putting the helmet on, he pushes my hands away and fixes the strap before climbing on himself and doing what he did last night. He pulls me close to his body so I'm like a vine wrapped around a tree. I feel him blow out a deep breath and tension leaves his body when I rest my head against his strong back and run my fingers over his hard stomach.

"Easy, Babe."

He grunts and I giggle when my fingers brush over his jean covered cock. Before I can say anything, he kicks the bike to life and the rumble of the pipes echoes around us.

**Drake**

After parking the bike, Harlow pushes off my shoulders and makes quick work of the helmet. She turns and takes a couple of steps away. Fuck that, I need to know what the hell is going on.

I pull Harlow's hand back towards me and she stumbles a little, her hands land on my shoulders and I grip her waist, flexing my fingers into her soft flesh, satisfied when I hear the hitch in her breath. "Babe, talk to me."

"Can't this wait?" She glances over her shoulder, a look crossing her face that I don't understand.

"Talk to me." My voice is softer, deeper now.

"Fine." She turns back to me, but her eyes are locked on my cut.

Placing two fingers under her chin, I tilt her head back until her eyes lock with mine. For the first time in my life, I see utter heartbreak in her dark eyes and my heart does some funny shit in my chest. She blinks a few times and I know she's fighting back tears. I swear to the Devil himself, I will break whoever did this to her.

"My sister," she breathes out softly, but when she speaks next, all traces of hurt and vulnerability wash away and the hard girl I first met is standing in front of me. "My sister was murdered two months ago. The last thing I know is she worked here and was dating a guy named Elliot." She pauses a moment to let that sink in. "That piece of shit in the club is the only lead I have in finding out what happened to my sister. I've bided my time. I got a job in this place to work out who he was."

"Why didn't you ask Trevor who he was before today?" Something doesn't add up.

"After the day I got the job he was never around, I thought I could figure it out for myself but it was a bust. I knew the Charity party was coming up and knew in my bones that

Trevor would be here along with the piece of shit who killed my sister." She blows out a deep breath before running her tongue across her bottom lip while she contemplates something.

"What is it?" I ask.

"At first I thought he was a part of the MC, but now, I just don't know."

"I can tell you one thing for sure, the MC might not be completely legitimate but we don't hurt women or children. It's a line *none* of us cross." My tone is as hard as steel.

I need her to believe what I'm saying. She looks at me with hard eyes for a few beats before they soften and I let go of the breath I didn't realise I was holding, knowing she gets it.

"So, can we go in?"

Leaning forward, I brush my lips over hers before pulling back and letting go of her waist. I grab her hand tightly in mine so she doesn't take off. Her shoulders slump when she realises I'm not letting her go. I push off my bike and rise to my full height.

"Lead the way, Lemon Drop."

"Can I have my hand back?" she grumbles.

I don't say a word, instead, I squeeze my fingers with hers and nod towards the doors. No fucking way am I letting her go. I get what she needs to do but she won't be doing it without me.

"Fine," she grumbles but squeezes my fingers with hers.

Just as we hit the doors, Alexis comes running across the road with her phone held to her ear.

"Harlow, wait," she calls out.

I look over her head and see Razor is following.

"What?" Harlow spins around.

The motion causes my arm to wrap around her waist and I pull her back into my chest. I grit my teeth when I feel her lush as fuck ass rub up against me and my cock pushes against my zipper.

"Don't you have any control?" she mumbles so only I can hear her.

Leaning down, I nip her ear before sucking it into my mouth to ease the sting. Her body shudders.

"That one was *your* fault," I growl, making her bite back a laugh.

"Tilly's on the phone." Alexis puts her on loudspeaker.

"Harlow." A breathless voice sounds down the line.

"What's wrong?" Harlow answers. I feel her stiffen.

"I just wanted to say, I'm sorry I'm not there with you. Alexis filled me in so you go in there and kick that guys ass until we know what the hell happened to Julie."

Taking a deep breath, Harlow leans into me. I kiss the crown of her head and notice her eyes are closed. I run the thumb of my free hand under her eye when I see I single tear escape her eyelash. A slight smile graces her lips at the touch. Her spine stiffens and I know I have no need to worry, my girls got this.

"I love you," she says to the woman on the phone.

"I love ya, too" Tilly gets out before a guy's voice in the background calls out.

"That better be your fucking mother you're saying that to," he growls.

My eyebrows hit my hairline and my eyes dart to Razor who's staring at the phone, wide eyed.

"No fucking way," I mumble.

"What?" Harlow and Alexis whisper at the same time.

"Jace, you fucking caveman. Chill the fuck out," Tilly calls back.

I choke back a laugh at hearing our Prez being told off.

"I'll show you caveman. Hang up that fucking phone, Tilly, unless you want them to hear me spank your ass."

Tilly squeals.

"Call me," Tilly rushes out before the phone clicks off.

"Well, fuck me," Razor huffs.

I nod, I never thought the day would come.

"Can someone please clue me in on what the fuck that was about?" Harlow demands while Alexis nods in agreement.

"Jace is the President of the Deadly Sins MC. Nobody, well nobody who's still alive, talks to him like that." I chuckle and rake my free hand through my hair.

"She's safe, right?" Alexis' voice is laced with worry.

"Yeah babe, Prez wouldn't touch a hair on her head." Razor reassures her before throwing an arm around her shoulders.

"But, he will spank her ass," Harlow throws out.

She bites her lip in an attempt not to laugh, it doesn't help and we all crack up.

"She's safe." I again reassure Alexis but I can't help but chuckle.

"Come on, Babe, let's get this shit done and we can head to the clubhouse where the Prez will be with your friend. You can see for yourself."

Harlow laughs. "Um... I don't think I wanna see that."

She smiles up at me before we head towards the door of Club Ivy. I give her ass a slap, giving her a taste of what's to come tonight after the stunt she pulled today.

***

"Shadow," I bark.

Looking around, I don't see him on the main floor. I turn towards Razor and raise an eyebrow in question.

"He said he was here." He shrugs.

"Shadow, where the fuck are you?" I shout.

"Chill, VP." He chuckles as he appears from a back room, Joel and Pete by his side.

"Where is he?"

"He needed to cool the fuck down so, we put him in the coolroom." He grabs a tea towel from the bar and wipes his hands.

"Prospects, go grab the motherfucker and let's get this shit sorted."

At their VP's command, Joel and Pete spin around and head back to where they came from.

While Razor takes care of introductions, I head to the bar and snatch a bottle of scotch from the glass shelf. I grab a single glass after the girls say no to my offer of a drink and pour a decent amount. I place the cap back on top and the bottle back on the shelf at the same time the Prospects throw a shivering Elliot into the middle of the dance floor.

"Grab a chair," I call out.

Joel steps to the side, grabs a sturdy wooden chair and sticks it next to the piece of shit.

"Wanna tell me what this is all about?" Elliot spits out through chattering teeth.

"I see you haven't learnt any manners since last night." I click my tongue and shake my head.

"Pete, put him on the chair."

"Don't fucking touch me," he snarls. Less than a second later, a loud crack sounds around the room. Picking my glass up, I walk to the other side of the bar and lean against the smooth wood. I take a mouthful while watching as Shadow shakes out his hand.

"Motherfucker has no respect and a boney ass jaw," Shadow grumbles.

The girls bite their lips trying not to laugh and I take another mouthful of drink.

"Babe." I nod towards Elliot and watch as his eyes take her in from head to toe. A loud growl escapes my throat and I take a step towards him before Harlow moves in front of me. Leaning up, she places a kiss on my lips.

"I've got this." Steel laces her voice and my cock throbs in my pants.

Leaning around me, she reaches over the bar and grabs something before turning back to Elliot. She plays with a stainless-steel ice pick between her fingers.

"Your fucked now," Shadow chuckles.

"Good luck with her," Pete says while squeezing the bastard's shoulder and chuckling.

The men take a few steps back so Harlow can approach.

"What the fuck do you want, you stupid slut?" He spits on the floor in front of her.

I start to move but Razor stops me with a hand on the chest. Swatting his hand away, I grunt and take a step forward. Alexis moves in front of me with her hands raised. She tilts her head to lock eyes with me and I see the plea.

"She needs to do this, Drake," she whispers. "Trust me, she can handle herself. Please?"

After a moment, I nod in understanding. The heartbreak I saw in her eyes outside gnaws at me. I know I have to let this play out for Harlow's sake. As much as it pisses me off and I should be the one to take care of this, I remind myself, she needs this. Blowing out a deep, frustrated breath, I nod again. My eyes snap up when the asshole screams out in pain. My girl has stabbed him in the thigh with the pick and she begins twisting it.

"Now is that anyway to talk to a lady?"

"Fuck you," he spits through gritted teeth.

"I think we already went over this, but if you need another lesson I'm sure I can teach you." She rips the pick free in one smooth move.

"Son of a bitch," he hisses out.

"What the fuck do you want?" he wheezes out after a moment and several deep breaths. He arches his neck away from Harlow when she runs the pick across his throat.

"Tell me what you did to my sister." Harlow places the end of the pick against his shoulder blade and starts to twist.

"Shit," Joel mumbles and covers his mouth as he chuckles. Looking over at Pete, I note the fascination and awe written all over his face as he watches my woman. It pisses me off and I squeeze my fists together. I try to concentrate on what's going on before I slam their faces into the hardwood floor.

"Who's your sister?" Elliot wheezes while watching the pick sink into his flesh in a little deeper.

"Her name is Julie. She's one of the softest souls you could ever meet." Her voice is soft but strong.

"Oh, yeah. She was a tasty piece of ass, she begged to suck my cock every night!"

"Piece of shit." Harlow pulls the pick from his shoulder and before I can blink, she pulls her arm back and with force, stabs him the chest. He screams out in agony and fights against the ropes holding him in place. I hear soft crying and worry it's my girl but when I glance to my right, I see the tears running down Alexis' face. She's wrapped protectively in Razor's arms. I shift my focus back to my girl. I've had about enough of this, I take a few more steps forward.

"Wanna try again?" Harlow snarls.

"I didn't kill her," he moans.

"Then who?" Harlow lines up the end of the pick with his left eye, moving her hand slowly so he's sure to see it coming.

"Do you know how messy it can get if this punctures your eye? Not to mention the pain."

The pick is about a centimeter from his eye and I hear his breathing increase as he panics.

"I guess I don't have to stress about it too much. See that beast of a man over there?" She nods towards me.

I watch his eyes flicker to me before returning to her and he nods.

She lowers her head to his. "That man beast is *mine!*"

My chest swells and possession settles in every cell of my body.

"Sooo, if I make a mess, he'll get someone to clean it up for me." She clicks her tongue. "The pain? I guess that will be your problem now, won't it?"

The smile she gives him is downright sinister. I squeeze my hands into fists and feel my knuckles pop. I want nothing more than to throw her over my shoulder and take what's mine.

"Do you wanna know something?" she whispers, moving the pick so it's brushing his eyelashes. "You're going to die today, no matter what, but I'll let you decide by who, them...." she nods to us. "And they'll make it quick, or me and I'll take it nice and slow. All you have to do is, tell me who the fuck killed my sister and the boys will finish it. Your choice."

I'm so fucking turned on right now, I'm about to lose my fucking mind.

Harlow pushes the pick closer to his eye. "Brother... my brother! Fuck, it was my brother," he yells.

She grabs a fist full of hair and jerks back his head. "Where is he?"

"I don't know, I haven't seen him since that night. I owed him so, I gave him Julie as payment."

"You piece of SHIT!" she screams out.

Harlow stabs him in the eye, punches him several times in the face and brings her knee down hard on his balls. Finally, I move. I can't stand watching my girl break down in front of me. Grabbing her tight around the waist, I swing her up into my arms and pull her against my chest. Tears stream down her face and her breathing is shallow and choppy.

"I've got you, Babe." I kiss the crown of her head.

"Clean this place up and get rid of that piece of shit," I growl to the Prospects.

They nod in reply.

"Shadow, find everything you can on his piece of shit brother."

"On it, VP." He sprints to the steps leading up to the office.

"Razor, I need you to take Alexis either to her place or the clubhouse on your bike. My girl is in no condition to be on the back of my bike"

"I'm okay," Harlow whispers.

Looking down, I shake my head.

"Got it, VP," he says as I pass them heading for the front doors.

Alexis is almost as bad as Harlow and tears stream down her face.

"I got you, Babe." Razor is holding her close.

"Please take me to where Harlow is going," she sobs.

"Clubhouse," I call as I step outside.

"I've got you, Babe," I breathe into her hair.

Alexis races out and hands me the keys.

"Thanks, will you be okay?" I know what happened inside was a lot to take in.

"That piece of shit deserved everything he got in there and so much more." The anger in her voice takes me by surprise. "I just need Harlow to be okay," she says sadly.

"She will be."

"I know." Razor has joined us and wraps his arms around her.

"See you at home, VP." He lifts his chin before guiding Alexis towards his bike.

I head to Harlow's black *Jeep.*

"Thank you." Harlow's whispered words hit my chest.

"Babe, it was hard as fuck standing back, watching you. I'm the man, I should have done this shit for you." I blow out a hard breath. "I know you needed to do it, but from now on, it's you and me, Lemon Drop."

"Promise?"

We reach the car. I drop her legs to the ground, lean her against the car door, grip her hair in one hand and grab her ass in the other. I slam my mouth down on hers in a hard kiss, pouring everything I have into it. Pulling back, I suck her bottom lip into my mouth and taste the saltiness of her tears on my tongue.

"Always," I grunt.

Leaning up, she wraps her arms around my neck and pulls me down into an all-consuming kiss that nearly knocks me to my knees. Releasing her ass, I grip the top of her car to keep me standing. Pulling back and on a panted breath, I growl out so she understands how serious I am.

"You are my *Sin*, Lemon Drop. Fuck, I know it hasn't even been twenty-four hours, but I love you."

"I love you too, Drake."

Her dark, liquid eyes meet mine and what I see, settles everything I never knew was out of place, deep in my gut.

We didn't ask for this.

We were never looking for this.

But, nothing will stop me from keeping her.

She's MINE.

# Epilogue

***One week later...***

**Harlow**

*Got My Mind Set On You* by *George Harrison* blasts from the speakers and I do a little hop in my step. Loving this song and humming away, I lean across the bar to listen to the guys order in front of me. Nodding I turn and start fixing his order. After last week went down, Drake called a meeting with the members about what to do about *Club Ivy*. As Trevor was gone, they decided I was to run the place. I was skeptical at first, but I have to admit, I love it. I love having Alexis working with me too. She gave up her old job and being here has really opened her up. It doesn't hurt that she has the love of a good man at her side. I wink at her as she refills a guy's beer. She looks over my shoulder, laughs and shakes her head. I don't need to look, or be told, that my beast of a man is watching me. It doesn't matter where I am, when he's in the room, I feel his heavy stare following me and it sends my body into a frenzy.

Glancing over my shoulder, I wink at him. He's leaning against the end of the bar staring at me with hunger in his eyes. My body comes to life when his thick tongue darts out and swipes across his bottom lip. I suck my bottom lip into my mouth, wanting a taste of him. Returning to the guy awaiting his order, I slide his order in front of him. He pulls his money out to pay and holds it out. When I reach for the money, he grabs my hand. I attempt to tug away, but he leans across the bar to whisper something to me. He doesn't even get his mouth open before he finds himself in mid-air, being thrown backwards onto the floor. My man stands tall above him. Everyone stops what they're doing and they stare at the guy trying to climb to his feet. Thank fuck the place is mostly filled with bikers tonight and no-one tries to help the sleaze ball off the floor. Leaning down, Drake picks him up by the scruff of the shirt and spits something in his face before pointing over to me. I try to mask my smile at his jealousy. Drake drops him to the floor and gets Pete, one of the Prospects, to drag his ass out of the club. He then makes his way back over to me.

"Fuck Babe, every fucking guy," he grunts.

"I'm sure it's not *every* guy." I set a scotch on the bar for him.

He eyes me over the rim of the glass before throwing it back and grunting like a caveman, making me laugh.

"I know what will stop these fucks from thinking they can hit on my Ol' Lady."

"Yeah, Baby, what's that?" I lean across the bar on my elbows, a smirk curls my lips.

Leaning towards me, he grips my hair in his fist and slams his mouth down on mine, stealing my breath. I moan at the taste of cinnamon and scotch and swipe my tongue over his, needing more. Pulling back, he grunts out, "That!"

"What?" I ask, trying to get my brain to catch up.

He looks down at the bar and following his line of sight, I notice a package wrapped in brown paper that wasn't there before.

"What's this?" I raise my eyebrow at him.

"Fuck, Babe, just unwrap it," he grumbles, making me laugh.

Picking the package up, I bring it to my ear and give it a shake. I don't hear anything, not that I could anyways with the music blaring around us. Drake chuckles as I put it back on the bar and begin to unwrap it.

I gasp when I see what's in it and holding it up, I roll my eyes at what's written on the back. It's a leather cut. It's so soft, but that's not what has me rolling my eyes. On the back it reads - *Property of Mercy*. It's wrapped around the club's logo of a skull wearing a crown, across the forehead of the skull is written, *Deadly Sins MC*. Crossed bones lay behind the skull mixed with roses, two guns cross at the base. I fell in love with it the first time I saw it tattooed on Drake's back. So much so, that I asked Jace - the club President, if I could get the same tattoo on my lower back. He's booked me into *Xtreme Ink* on Darby Street next week to get it done.

Locking eyes with Drake, I slide it on. His features harden. The grip he has on the glass in his hand tightens. His knuckles turn white and the glass shatters.

"Fuck, Babe." I turn to grab a cloth for his hand, but before I can move, two hands reach over the bar. Next thing I know, I'm over his shoulder and he's striding through the club as cat calls ring out around us.

"Fuck, Babe, need inside you now." He's gone all caveman and shit.

He slaps my ass as he takes the stairs two at a time, my body shudders and locks at the sensation. I hear a door being kicked open and the next thing I know, my back hits a hard surface. I look around to see, we're in my office. Before I can say a word, everything on my desk goes crashing to the floor and he's sliding me up my desk, ripping my jeans off at the same time.

"Time to test out this desk and claim what's mine," he growls.

He tears my panties off with a snap and I hiss as the elastic breaks against my skin. Hearing the snap of his belt, my body hums with excitement.

"I'm going to fuck you through the floor, Lemon Drop and no one will ever doubt you're mine."

His mouth hits mine hard and he slams into me with one hard, smooth thrust which has me coming off the desk. I have to rip my mouth from his to catch my breath. Twisting his hand into my hair, he grips my hip and raises me a little so he can hit deeper. I can't stop the moans from slipping free.

"This is going to be fast, Babe. When I get you home, I'll take my time and devour every inch of you and give this greedy pussy everything it begs for."

"Fuck." His words and the way he's hitting my sweet spot with every thrust is sending me over the edge - fast.

"Every fucken time," he grits out on each thrust. "Come!"

That does it. My body flies and I'm sent into a world of endless colours as he slams into me one more time. His groans bounce off the walls around us and I feel his warm release shoot into my core, sending another set of spasms racing through me.

***

**Drake**

The best thing I ever did in my life, besides joining the MC, was making this woman mine. Nothing compares to the way she makes me feel. She is not only the light of my day, but she is also my dark. Because in the dark, we create enough light but as long as Harlow is here, I'll suck it the fuck up. Because, wearing my cut or not, the woman is MINE.

**THE END FOR NOW.....**

A 7 DEADLY SINS MC NOVEL
KAY MAREE

# Available exclusively at Amazon

Angel Mine (Mine #1) ~ Dominic & Brooklyn
Kitten Mine (Mine #2) ~ Antonio & Katherine
Sugar Mine (Mine #3) ~ Sergio & Kirsty
Petal Mine (Mine #3.5) ~ Nico & Josie
Trixie Mine (Mine #4) ~ Theo & Trinity (Coming Soon 2018)

# Other books by Kay Maree

Inked Temptation – Book 1 Inked Series
Shadow Game
Majestic (Midnight Crest Book 1)
Cherry Christmas ~ A Stone Brothers Trilogy

# Follow Links

**Facebook** - @KayMareeAuthor   **Twitter** - MisKay85
**Insta** - miskay
https://www.facebook.com/groups/AngelsKittensSugars/

https://kaymareesmutlover.wixsite.com/contemporary-romance

9 780648 390473